AF409041

Dhol

I dreamt of being in a theatre witnessing from the very beginning of creation of the universe, up till the end of the history of the world.

Solihin Yusoff

Copyright © 2019 Solihin Yusoff
All rights reserved

Acknowledgements

In the name of Allah, the most gracious, most merciful.

Without whom this intuition and inscriptions will never happen.

Peace be upon Rasullullah Muhammad [saw], for he a role model that mankind to be followed.

Several key people deserve all the thanks for the making of this book into reality.

Ana Solihin, my main support and beloved life partner till Jannah.

My daughters, Kamila and Umi, who tirelessly proof read and ghost write on several gaps and descriptions during late nights of their precious weekends and holidays.

My boys, Khalil, Noah and Ilham, coolness of my eyes whom inspired me to pen this storyline.

Dr Nouman Ali Khan is the priceless inspiration in so many parts of this write up.

Prof Dato' Dr Mohd Asri Zainul Abidin for his thoughts and provoking approach has widened my view on various perspective of Islamic practicalities.

Introduction

I dreamt of being in a theatre witnessing from the very beginning of creation of the universe, up till the end of the history of the world.

A true-life panorama evolution

The Rise and Fall of each civilization

Trailing each and every main character per generation

I wish them all be captured in a video form for playbacks, whenever and wherever I feel like.

I envisage a society living in heaven, perfectly harmonious serenity, with evil out of the script, in full definition.

I aspire to deepen most the contents of The Al-Mighty scriptures in entirety and relate each human's destructions and atrocities as it was written in His warnings and advises.

Through generations, mankind evolved to greatness at the expense of destruction and atrocities.

I ask myself: Are all these necessary?

If we equip ourselves with knowledge and a sense of humility, no necessity is a clear answer to the aforesaid.

If and only if we explore the root of our ancestors would we realize our immense

dependencies to the hidden Hand, The Al
Mighty.

Dol is in a mission to track his long-lost father
and twin brother. Throughout his journey of
quest, Dol stumbled upon unscripted incidents.
As a man who frequents the recitation of Al
Quran, Dol began to map the contents as was
written for generations before him and
observes on-goings before his eyes. Sadaqalahul
Adzim [Allah The Immense said true]. Men are
just NOT doing what God had guided them to
do. Too many destructions, wars, envies,
cruelties, hatred, greed, killings.

Dol is in the state of _Dhol_, an Arabic term describing a person in confusion.

And all from the hands of human. Dhol is
confused. As he recites a verse from Ad Dhuha
93:7, the word Dhol suited well in every inch of
his quest to find the truth. And that he prayed
for Allah Almighty to guide him along his way to
the righteous.

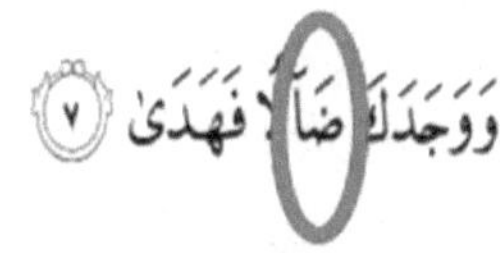

وَوَجَدَكَ ضَآلًّا فَهَدَىٰ ۝

" And He found you lost and guided [you],"

Hence his quest.................

Luqman 31:31

أَلَمْ تَرَ أَنَّ ٱلْفُلْكَ تَجْرِى فِى ٱلْبَحْرِ بِنِعْمَتِ ٱللَّهِ لِيُرِيَكُم مِّنْ ءَايَٰتِهِۦٓ إِنَّ فِى ذَٰلِكَ لَءَايَٰتٍ لِّكُلِّ صَبَّارٍ شَكُورٍ ۝

"Do you not see that ships sail through the sea by the favour of Allah that He may show you of His signs? Indeed, in that are signs for everyone patient and grateful."

Ar Ruum 30:9

أَوَلَمْ يَسِيرُوا۟ فِى ٱلْأَرْضِ فَيَنظُرُوا۟ كَيْفَ كَانَ عَٰقِبَةُ ٱلَّذِينَ مِن قَبْلِهِمْ كَانُوٓا۟ أَشَدَّ مِنْهُمْ قُوَّةً وَأَثَارُوا۟ ٱلْأَرْضَ وَعَمَرُوهَآ أَكْثَرَ مِمَّا عَمَرُوهَا وَجَآءَتْهُمْ رُسُلُهُم بِٱلْبَيِّنَٰتِ فَمَا كَانَ ٱللَّهُ لِيَظْلِمَهُمْ وَلَٰكِن كَانُوٓا۟ أَنفُسَهُمْ يَظْلِمُونَ ۝

Translation:
"Have they not travelled through the earth and observed how was the end of those before

them? They were greater than them in power, and they plowed the earth and built it up more than they have built it up, and they're messengers came to them with clear evidences. And Allah would not ever have wronged them, but they were wronging themselves."

Solihin Yusoff
04 January 2019
Shah Alam
Malaysia

Dedication

To my beloved and dear parents,

Allahyarham Haji Yusoff and Allahyarhamah Hajah Chik.

For the years you spent raising my siblings and I, your sacrifices, dedication, care and love.........

May your souls rest in peace, and that all your deeds accepted by Allah [Subhanahu Wa Ta'ala].

Al Baqarah 2:156

ٱلَّذِينَ إِذَآ أَصَٰبَتْهُم مُّصِيبَةٌ قَالُوٓا۟ إِنَّا لِلَّهِ وَإِنَّآ إِلَيْهِ رَٰجِعُونَ ﴿١٥٦﴾

"Who, when disaster strikes them, say, " Indeed, we belong to Allah, and indeed to Him we will return."

Al Fatihah.

Aamiin ya rabbal alamin

Chapter 1 - Serendip

The sun has risen half past the sea level.

The wind breezes calmly, creating soft ocean tides and drifting shells to the shore.

A flock of wedge-tailed shearwaters began chirping while entering coastal waters of Serendip Island situated at the tip of the southern India sub-continent.

Footsteps of 5 men walking along the beach grew louder as they drew nearer to the waters.

The tallest of the men, signalled to another group on horses at higher grounds at some distance away, as if he needed some extra time to investigate a new discovery.

There lies a body of a man laying faced down that seemed lifeless. The men stood there for some moments.

With his left hand holding a mid-sized riding crop, the shortest man poked at the immobile body.

"Wake up, bhai," he said in a thick Hindustani accent.

Dhol finds it so hard to open his eyes.

This has been his worst nightmare ever in his entire life. He thought he was dead, entering the realm of the afterlife...........

As he slowly opened his eyes, the tall man puts a thumbs-up to the group at the higher ground," He's alive, alright."

In Dhol, every joint of his body felt stiff and frozen, too difficult to move. He turned his neck to the left and saw his small notebook lying an inch away from his left foot.

He struggled but managed to reach for the book and slid it under his pocket. Fortunately, none of the men noticed as one of them started to talk while the rest too focused on the words uttered by the man talking.

He tried to move his body but they're hurting all over, as if he was a glowstick that had been bent and crushed at every inch. Dhol groaned in pain.

Looking at the ocean, some parts of his tiny vessel wreckage were afloat not far away from the shore.

Tears began to flow from his eyes." My dream is now shattered," Dhol said to himself, softly.

"What language is he speaking?" asked the tall man to another.

The man next to the tall one shrugged off his shoulders, the others did the same.

Dhol took a while to bring himself up on his knees while looking at some debris being washed to the shore.

Dhol then said," It's Malay, but if you prefer Arabic, Persian or Hindustani, I can as well," in formal Hindustani.

"How did you end up here?" the smallest man asked further. "Bad weather. From Malacca, en-route to Mecca," replied Dhol.

"What is that mark on your right back shoulder blade?". To that Dhol said, "Just my birthmark." The smallest man came closer and stared at Dhol's birthmark. He then walked to Dhol's front and held his face by the chin tightly with his left hand. He turned Dhol's face left and right several times. He paused for a while. Then did it again and again. "Stand up!" said the smallest man, waving his right hand as a signal for Dhol to stand up. The other 2 men lifted Dhol up, whom seemed reluctant to obey. For he truthfully is still weak from the storm hard hit earlier. As Dhol slowly raise, the tallest man got closer to him. As Dhol straightened his body up, it turns out that he is just slightly taller than Dhol by a hair line. He then made a swift turn, held Dhol's waist from behind and clutch it firmly. He then stood very close with Dhol at his left. It is as if he is measuring Dhol's height. "Hmmmm," the small man sigh with astonishment.

The smallest man then stepped behind a distance away and pulled the tallest of the men to a corner. They spoke for a moment while glancing to Dhol every now and then. The other 3 men stood by on guard near Dhol, as if he had committed a crime. Dhol couldn't make out what they were discussing about.

The tallest man later shouted to the caravan, "We're taking him!" hence getting a waving hand from a man on a white horse, standing in the middle of the group at the hilltop some half a mile away.

Dhol struggled to stand up when, *dupp.* A loud thud followed by a burst of pain on his left eye and cheek. He fell. Everything went dark.

Chapter 2 - The Sail

Just several days earlier, away in the West Coast port of Malacca, Dhol had caught a super large sword fish. He made good money from the sale of it, valued worth more than several months of savings into his coffers, with just this one catch. He then sold his mid-size blue-ish wooden fishing boat along with his fishing tackles to a known wealthy local broker for a handsome amount.

"Ahh, Umi will be pleased. I have enough money to start my journey now," he quipped to himself, smiling while heading towards home. Several young girls nearby seemed to have a good glimpse of Dhol as he passed by the market. Dhol was 6 foot 1, a little slouched with wide shoulders and a broad chest. At 30, he's wise at sea. With his prominent nose, a cleft chin, and husky voice, he's the man of many women's dreams as far as physical is the main criteria. Dhol picked up Arabic, Persian and Hindustani languages from his daily contacts of merchants he met during trades of his daily fishing catches.

At Syuruk the next morning, as Dhol was folding several pieces of clothes into his sling rug at his traditional Malay wooden house by the sea, a knock on the front door several times broke the silence. "Assalamualaikum, Dhol," a husky and deep voice called from outside. "Waalaikumsalam. I'll be ready in no time, PakSu," Dhol greeted an elderly man in his 70's as he removed the house front door latch. PakSu waited a moment, then handed him a well packed lemang and beef rendang. PakSu knows that lemang and rendang are Dhol's favorite meal, usually prepared by Dhol's mom, Umi. But not this time. Umi is no longer around. It was only a week ago that Umi was laid to rest at the burial ground adjacent to the mosque in his village.

 "This can last for several days. I will always pray for you, my dear son," PakSu uttered. "PakSu, I aim to be back by the next 2 Ramadhans. Please help to look after this house while I'm away. Assalamualaikum," while kissing PakSu's hand and hugging him. Dhol then bowed down and began to gather his packs to leave.

 Several men around Dhol's age, dressed in Baju Melayus and clad in chapals, waited patiently by the staircase. "Thank you, comrades. Without your encouragements, guidance and teachings,

I will not have the guts to leave Malacca." His childhood friends accompanied him to the port with him and PakSu leading the way.

PakSu is the village head, and also his uncle - his mother, Umi's younger brother. PakSu was religiously responsible for Dhol's upbringing. Pak Su has been in his life, for as long as he could remember -- since he can recall, when his dad left and never returned.

PakSu patted Dhol's shoulder while walking along. PakSu decided to lead the path rather than leave Dhol to walk alone to the port. The friends followed as well. "Ayah has a deep scar just below his left cheek from the bamboo arrow accident when we were young. I don't think that scar can easily disappear even after many years on. Dhol remembers well of PakSu's description of his father.

"Ayah" as in father is the most common term in Malay language. Ayah was about Dhol's height. Similar to his body structure and with cleft chin. As for the identical younger twins, he has the same blue black oval shaped birthmark as you on his right back shoulder blade. About the size of your pinky. "These are all that I can recall. Use these to identify them." Reminded PakSu.

As for Ayah's friend, PakSu only calls him Pak Syeikh and never knew his real name. But he reminded Dhol that Pak Syeikh was about Ayah's age of reaching 70, he hailed from somewhere in middle east origin, but I wasn't sure which part. He was a slick businessman wIth fluent Malay apart from his native. He has green eyes.

PakSu tapped onto Dhol's shoulder, which brough Dhol back from the deep thoughts he was in. "I was told by an old friend, a seaman, based on his previous trip, that the vessel that you are getting into will settle down circa Gulf of Eden port in Yemen in 2 months' time. From there you have to ride on the camel heading northwest crossing the Arabian peninsular towards Mecca. The ride will take you slightly over a month, given the summer condition as you arrive. You will travel during the night, and rest during the day. Your challenge is to find a middle-aged clerk named Haji Abu in Eden to assist when you get there". Pausing for a while, PakSu continued, " And, here's a collection from the villagers for your safe journey," while tucking in several dinar coins into Dhol's palm. Dhol was touched with the contribution but held his emotions to himself.

Dhol glanced back to wave to PakSu and his childhood friends. Now standing a mile away from his home, he turned around and pictured his mother standing at the doorway, looking at him and wiping away her tears with the sleeve of her green baju kurung. "I will bring Ayah and twin brother home, Umi", he said to himself.

The double deck vessel is now within a stone's throw away from where he is standing. "Bismillah hi tawakkal al Allah", Dhol uttered as he continues his walk towards the deck.

Chapter 3 - Captive

Dhol felt a sharp pain on his left eye when he finally woke up. He scanned his surrounding and quickly gathered that he's in a moving, rectangle wooden carriage along with three other men. Thin rays of light seep through the small windows on the sides of the carriage. He sees that they are passing through some sort of forest. From the sound of hooves clacking on the ground, Dhol could make out that the carriage was being led by horses.

He wanted to move closer to the windows to get a better view of the outside, but was restricted by chains that tied his ankles to the pole that stood right next to him. He realised that all the other captives were in a similar situation – while tied to the pole, they were either sitting down on the poorly assembled wooden planks that make the base of the carriage, or standing up, leaning against their pole, gazing hopelessly out the window.

As his mind reached more and more clarity since waking up, Dhol began to question, *who are these people? Where are they taking me?*

*Why was I captured? Where am I? Why me?
How long have I been in here?*

"Aaatcchhuummm", a captive man sitting just a few inches to his right sneezed. He is so burly that Dhol can hardly see the skin on his back. His pungent smell is nothing less than cow dung. He must have been tied to the pole for some time by now. He is about Dhol's height but skinnier with curly hair and wearing only a pair of torn pants. "Idiot, what are you staring at?" the man hurled at Dhol. The smell coming out of his mouth reeked so badly, Dhol couldn't take it any longer and puked several times. At this moment, he took the poorly assembled flooring planks as a blessing. With cracks and small gaps between the planks, his vomit escaped to the moving ground underneath the carriage.

Apart from burly man, Dhol took notice of two other men in the carriage. Instead of sitting down, they were standing up. They were smaller and shorter in size, so their heads were a good hands-reach below the roof of the carriage. They were also visibly younger than him. He said nothing to them. Everyone stared at each other. Dhol looks like the freshest and cleanest of all.

A voice from outside the cage can be heard asking someone," how many more days before we reach there?". Another man replied, "Today we will reach the base, another three to the middle of the mountain. Then we go on foot to reach the base camp. The prisoners will be taken out from the carriage and walk along with us." After a brief pause, the rider continued, "That's Adam's Peak alright", as he pointed with his left hand towards the mountain.

Dhol and the other men look at each other. Through the small windows, Dhol can clearly see the top of the huge natural structure, though the day is getting darker. From within the cage, the so-called prisoners continued to listen to the conversation of the guards, as they recalled the history of the mountain.

"So, tell me who is Adam of this peak?" asked one of the guards. The bigger-sized guard replied," I don't know, but I heard it got its name from the first man created by god. Adam was thrown out of heaven and landed on earth there. The Moslems, Christians, Jews, they all call him Adam." He continued, "Adam's footstep is still there and now carved in stones and ornamented with a single margin of brass and studded with gems."

The conversation reminded Dhol of the stories his uncle, PakSu, used to tell him. PakSu said that Adam, the father of all mankind and also the first prophet for the Moslems, had disobeyed God's instructions so he was banished from heaven and sent to earth, where he cried and repented for many years. "So, this must be the peak that PakSu was referring to," he thought. Perhaps God has scripted this path for me so I would have the opportunity to visit and witness the historical remains of our forefathers.

The carriage came to halt about an hour later. It was time for dinner and night rest for the travellers.

Chapter 4 - In the Cell

"Duupp", the sound of a hard drop to the ground. A coconut just fell from some fifty feet tree in the early morning. Thanks to Mr. Squirrel for the assistance. Dhol and the rest of the captives can only watch from the cage, despite their thirst. The coconut tree is just as similar to those back home. One of the guards picked up the coconut and started to drink its juice from within the cracks from the fall.

Dhol is still puzzled as to why and how he ended up in this cell with the rest, but can't seem to get an answer. The smallest, shortest, and probably the youngest of the prisoners looks more compromising to talk to compared with the other two. But he is farthest from Dhol. "Abang," whispered the small guy to Dhol. "What a relief," Dhol whispered to himself, having met someone this early in his journey that can speak Malay on a soil away from his homeland. It appears that the small guy speaks fairly good Malay like Dhol. Ilham, the boy was later known as, further said, "I heard from the riders that your vessel was wipe-washed by the typhoon. You passed out for several days after a hard punch from one of the guards. I'm glad you are still alive." He added, "Listen, I was born and raised on this Serendip Island. My grandparents are Malay merchants who travelled from Malacca 90 years ago and have settled here since then. Putting me in this cell was a big mistake by those men. My brother saw me getting caught by these cults. He is getting my dad and the villagers for help. Rescue will arrive soon."

Dhol looked at the other two. A mid aged fair complexion, prominent nosed man noticed Dhol was observing, then turned to him. He introduced himself as Kamil, a Moor from Al Andalus, a traveller, historian and an avid book collector based in Cordoba, apparently ended up here after being robbed of his business proceeds by pirates just before landing at the bottom tip of the island, just several days before Dhol. With no money, but wanting to return home, he opted to be a temporary slave, as long as he can reach home for free. Kamil is very proud of his homeland. And super proud of his knowledge on civilizations that he had come across during his travel worldwide. " Name me any civilizations, I can relate discoveries of the nations and its people. And I love to share this with all," he added.

It was at this moment that the large, burly guy interfered. "Be prepared with your stories. When your turn comes, you will be cleansed before he receives your audience. Whatever you share with my master Sam, it must contain good lessons. And that is if you are to survive."

Dhol became confused. He doesn't understand what these folks are talking about. Too many questions circling in his head. Who is this master Sam? Why the stories? What is with this master Sam that the prisoners have to be executed? Then Dhol remembered his tiny note book that he had brought along from home. That book has been with him since he was seven. His uncle PakSu was his great teacher. He learnt all his religious knowledge and tricks and trades of life from his very uncle. Despite his feet being chained to the pole, both his hands are free. "It could do some good help here then," he said to himself while trying to search the tiny book in his hidden pouch at his back pocket. "O Al Mighty, You and only You can save me and the rest". The book is still in his pocket intact.

"I heard master Sam likes to read but can't be certain of his major interest," continued the burly friend. Dhol was later made to understand that his new friend's name is Noah. He hails from Armenia, a mountainous area between the borders of Byzantine territory in the west and Persia in the east. Noah is very proud of his origin. But he refused to share a single hint of what fable he has in store for master Sam. He promised that master Sam will learn great lessons from his stories, and that he will be released upon the journey passing through his hometown of Mount Ararat.

"I must find out what is making everyone preparing for stories for master Sam. And I must prepare for my survival. But how, and who will help me?......

Chapter 5 - Coconuts

The tall chief guard that found Dhol lying at the beach was Karl. The prisoners heard the guards mentioning him earlier before his arrival at the cage. Karl had instructed the guards to give a bunch of coconuts for the prisoners as to show his humility. Saliva flowing from the mouths of Dhol and gang. One of the guards removes the chains that keeps the cage enclosed, and threw the coconuts into the cell. "Catch! Figure out how to get the juice yourself," the guard said while tossing a freshly picked green shelled ball to each of the prisoners. As the prisoners caught their coconuts, Karl observed their reactions. No one uttered a single word. Karl continued to glance around the cell, showing subtle concern for their conditions and well-being.

All the prisoners' faces are brimming with delight. It's like being invited to a feast for only the privileged few. "Here, let me show you my skills", quipped Ilham to the rest. "I'm a local, grew up with them and knew the tricks." He tapped, then shook the coconut that was tossed to him earlier. "Looks just young enough with sweet tender meat and watery juice," he said.

He looked around him, then placed the coconut with the flatter end facing downwards, in between the two flooring planks he was standing on. With just one strike of his left foot heel, the coconut juice shoots out upward from the shell like a fountain. "Tarra! That's how you do it," he said while slurping the juice.

 "Ahh, that is kiddy's way", replied Noah aka Mr. Hairy. "Here is the gentleman way," he continued. Noah held one coconut in his left hand. He then looked at Kamil, grabbed the coconut from the Moorish man, and held it in his right palm. With the other coconut in his left palm, Noah smashed both coconuts with just one bang. "Woosshh," both coconuts cracked with the juice splashed out like fountains. "There you go. We can both enjoy our drinks now." he winked to Kamil.

 With all three prisoners enjoying their drinks, all eyes are on Dhol. "Show us what technique you are going to use to get the juice and meat out", challenged Noah, the hairy man. Dhol smiled. He placed the fruit with the flat side at the bottom on the plank where he is standing. He kneeled down. With a little focus to aim the right angle, Dhol cracks open the fruit with an elbow swing to the top of the coconut. He then quickly poked the coconut top with his index finger and turned the fruit upside down. The juice flowed out from the poked point and straight down his throat without any wastage fallen to the ground. The other three prisoners were mesmerised by his prowess style. "Wow, you are indeed a professional," hairy man said while tapping Dhol on his shoulder. The other two guys clapped in agreement. Dhol had earned their respect.

That morning, the cage, the coconuts, the skills, and the tender meat, marked the beginning of a new friendship. An unexpected bond formed across individuals with very different backgrounds.

About an hour later, Karl returned with the guards and unlocked the cage. "Everyone, get out", a guard ordered. "Time to clean yourselves before heading to the mountain." Another guard stepped into the cage, pulled out a master key from his belt and removed all chains from the prisoners. Dhol couldn't remember the last time he had set foot on the ground. For the past a week and a half, all he was able to see was the passing scenery on either side of the carriage through the small windows. Upon stepping out of his cell, he realised that there are several other carriages in front of his. Imprisoned within them, were some ten other prisoners.

"Why do we have to walk?" wondered Dhol to himself. Ilham came close to Dhol and started to walk along with him. "Master Sam is a sick man. He doesn't sleep well since his wife died a year ago. A wise man advised him to visit Adam's Peak to be cured. He travelled all the way from Gorkha Kingdom in the north-east of India to seek treatment up there. He was told that by regretting, repenting, seeking for forgiveness, and saying his prayers there it would be accepted. And this is where he is taking us along with. Master Sam has done too much evil to his wife that she died of mental torture and sufferings. Even God's first-created man repented and sought for forgiveness at that peak." I was told that God had forgiven Adam after many years of repentance." Ilham continued, "But you know, I also heard that if master Sam feels that he is not feeling the intuition of God's forgiveness, he is going for plan B. And that is the reason why we are captured."

Dhol looked straight up to the mountain. He is getting more confused. If a person wants to repent, why would he capture this many innocent people along the way?........

Chapter 6 - The Escapade

The journey doesn't feel like it was that torturous. Prisoners walked in pairs, both hands tied behind their backs with a thick gunny rope linking each pair by their wrists. Dhol continued the mountain climb, paired with hairy Noah. They were the last in line. Deep said that their walk had covered almost two thirds of the journey to the peak with master Sam potentially having already reached his destination. But neither Dhol nor his new friends have seen how master Sam looks like.

Dhol had been observing the troops and the prisoners' behaviours since the start of the walk. He can easily untie the rope and escape from the crowd. The riders are too busy talking to each other. Those at the front are too far ahead from his visibility. As a fisherman, he learned a great deal on how to tie ropes for his boat, the fish, and tents. He is only looking for the right moment to pursue his plan. He needs to be extra careful as he is in a foreign land, a completely alien area. He can't figure out where his escape would lead him to.

    As they came across a right turn surrounding the hilly mountain, Dhol spotted a small passage the size of his body that he can easily slip into. Guards on bullock carts will surely not notice his disappearance if he sneaks away quick enough. By now, his rope is already untied without Noah even realizing it. As they approached the right corner, a prisoner somewhere in the front accidentally tripped and fell. The prisoner shouted in pain for an unknown reason. All eyes were focused on the incident. It was at this moment that Dhol pulled the string and broke away from the convoy. Within a few seconds, he was already in the passage entrance. Noah noticed but couldn't say a word before Dhol vanished from his sight. It was an entrance to a cave that was partly covered by hanging weeds. Dhol slipped and fell a few metres into the dark cave. He didn't look back, running straight ahead, stepping on some small stones along the way. As he went further, it appears that the cave is quite a one yoyo hilly passage. He could see a tiny light at the end of the tunnel. "I have nothing to lose, I have no clue where I am going, but this is the only chance I have." Off he went heading towards the direction where the light is coming from.

Dhol continued his run, falling several times in the dark with no help from slippery and wet grounds. Not a sign of the riders chasing him was heard. Not even Noah's footsteps, potentially wanting to join his escapade, he thought to himself. He was almost reaching the end of the passage now without any threats. "I am doing good. Good job Dhol," patting himself for the great escape achievement.

Dhol peeped outside, so curious of his whereabout, and tracking any signs of danger. He creeped out of the cave, having bled his elbows and knees from the fall earlier.

It sounded so peaceful with only birds chirping can be heard. Dhol cracked a long hanging branch that crossed his path. He used it as a staff for both protection and support. He is now a liberated man again.

As he searched for tropical fruits along the path, it led Dhol closer to the edge of the mountain. Dhol suddenly felt his knees weak. His movement seemed super slow. His ears can only hear a deep growl.

A panther is within striking distance. Dhol can see that the panther is moving towards him but not in a way of in search of food. Yet, Dhol's sweat began dripping from every part of his body. Will he surrender to this fiery, fanged creature, or roll down the 2,000 meters mountain cliff?

Dhol remembered he once followed his uncle to the jungle of Gunung Tahan, the largest central secondary forest in Peninsular Malay states. PakSu's words remained clear in his mind on how to survive when confronted by the larger cat families. With PakSu's voice in mind, Dhol performed the rituals in steps despite panting, but in control of his breath. Dhol tried to make himself appear larger by raising his arms. Dhol should not run as doing so may stimulate the panther to chase. He had to stand and face the animal. He had to stay firm with his eye contacts. Dhol stood there with very slow movements. He knew he couldn't keep much longer, but one small error would cause him his life. The panther starred, and so did Dhol. That moment of staying still felt like a year of standing and starring for Dhol. Warm water started to drip from Dhol's in-between legs. He knew. But he couldn't do much. Something else is more important that warrants his attention for now. One has to give in. They both stayed starring into each other's eyes for a while longer.

" I'm just passing by, no intention of encroaching your territory. I mean no harm," Dhol said firmly, surely.

As he stood facing the creature for some more 30 seconds, the Panther started to look elsewhere. Dhol's guess is true as the panther doesn't seem to be that hungry. The Panther slowly walks away and disappeared from his sight. "That was close, so close," Dhol sigh.

Dhol sat kneeling at the edge of a cliff nearby, looking at the surrounding. A waterfall is not far from where he stood. The wind blew towards the thick jungle, wetting some leaves from the waterfall. Dhol took a sip to drink from one of the leaves within his reach. He was too tired to continue his run. The night came early for him that day, he fell asleep within seconds.

Chapter 7 - Stupid

Splash...woosh. "Wake up, you stupid fool", the small local prisoner, Ilham, commanded in disgust while kicking Dhol with his left foot. "You think you are smart enough to escape, huh? You ended up only to reach the peak earlier instead." Dhol opened his eyes. All the new friends are standing around him with the guards holding batons, ready to blast Dhol's brain for his attempt to run away.

Dhol was lucky enough. Two guards from the front group turned back and approached the small crowd on their horses and said, "Let's keep the penalty for later till we reach the base camp. We are running late in time. Master Sam wants no injuries from now on to anyone as he prefers to focus on his prayers", said one of them. To that, Dhol was spared from any beatings. And he is back in the group for a journey to the unknown.

....

....

The journey is nearing to the base of Adam's peak. A Malay proverb would describe the distance as "Se tanak Nasi" similarly as "A time sufficient to cook a pot of rice", an estimate of fifteen to twenty minutes time to destination location.

Dhol regretted his act of stupidity though he still regards it as a brave one. He walked with his head down.

"Listen here. You wanted to travel to Mecca in search of your dad. But you have lost all your savings. This is a trip for you to get to your destination for FREE. I am just like you. We've lost our money. It is an opportunity that I would not miss, if I were you." Whisper Kamil giving some words of wisdom to Dhol. "But this is not Mecca!" replied Dhol. "Haish, I heard from the guards that a wise man told master Sam that he must repent and cleanse himself for all the cruelty he had done to his wife. According to historians, the father of mankind, Adam, regretted for not obeying God's instruction to not eat the fruit from the forbidden tree and listening to Satan. As a result, Adam ended up being thrown along with Eve to earth. Adam landed here. He blamed himself for losing Eve too. He repented here for many years until he received signal from God that his repentance was accepted. Adam then travelled to Mecca in search of Eve, only to be reunited in Jabbal Rahmah." continued Kamil. "What about us then?" asked Dhol. "Master Sam is suffering from a chronic insomnia. He has not slept well for a year since his wife's passing. To cure himself, he believes bedtime stories would help. But he doesn't want to listen to just any fairy tale stories. He'd like to learn and deepen his knowledge with stories of important lessons in life that he can improve his life towards. Hence taking along those he thinks are helpful to narrate the untold stories of the great. You can certainly benefit the least, if not more. So, stop thinking of escaping. Start planning to give, and share for the benefit of others." To that, the journey has reached its destination.

It is time for a night rest. Tomorrow will be a day to witness the steps of the first man on earth.

Chapter 8 - Insomnia

Dhol had just given his salaam which ends the early morning prayer when it started to drizzle. He peeped from the cell to see if the soil has any puddle that might affect any of the crops they had just planted. He can't see much as the clouds are still thick and the cold wind is blowing towards his cart cell direction, some leaves flying into it.

Noah is far from awake, switching sleeping sides while scratching his beard. Kamil is completely covered by his blanket from head to toe. Ilham the local boy, not a sign of waking up. The crop and small farm had been the food supply that master Sam and his crew survived on. The prisoners were forced to work on the soil to produce vegetables, potatoes, tapioca, and fruits. Rice is purchased at the foot of the mountain from the locals.

It has been 3 months since they occupied the small plot of land just at the base surrounding the stairs heading to the footprint monument at Adam's Peak. It has been also 3 months of Dhol and his mates observing master Sam commuting from his white tent to the peak weekly. Master Sam usually starts his 5,000 over steps climb very early in the morning. They say that it takes some 3 hours to reach the peak from the base where the group is located.

There are times when master Sam stayed there throughout the day, returning only the following day. At times, back to his base tent by same evening to rest. But not a single day that master Sam was seen or spotted sleeping any longer than 1 hour, as far as any of the travelling community guards had noticed. "Indeed Hypersomnia. Probably a very chronic one. No one can pretend to not sleep for such a long period as in the case of master Sam. Yet he can still climb the stairs steadily without much difficulty. Master Sam must not be that old," exclaimed Dhol. He kept wondering how it could be solved for a man who has everything in life, but could not find a cure for his own problem. Dhol wished that he could meet face to face with master Sam. Had a talk to understand more. He probably can offer master Sam his ears as a listener. Probably a good one, with the hope to ease off his burden and whatever that is kept in master Sam's mind and heart.

At almost midday, Dhol walked to the plantation area to check on the soil that has been damaged by the rain. It was quite close to master Sam's tent. The tent had a section of it with a semi-transparent curtain where you can see the person inside, though not that clear. Dhol had forgotten that master Sam decided not to take the stairs for the day. Dhol saw a man in his master's tent, seated on a prayer mat, with both legs folded Yoga style. He had a small book with him. Curiosity sparked. Dhol had never seen what master Sam looks like. He tried many times throughout the 3 months but hasn't had a single chance to glance at the master's face.

  From the back, Master Sam had the similar size and height as Dhol. His hair is, the least, shoulder long. A well-dressed man, master Sam could be also hiding himself from something else. Dhol realised that every time he was within a close range, master Sam would quickly cover his face with his large turban cloth. Sometimes, master Sam would turn his face to other directions and let his hair loose to cover his face. Of late, as his beard grew thicker and longer, it is not even possible to see his mouth except to hear his voice when talking.

In the wake of silence, Ilham came from nowhere, jolted Dhol from his daydream by poking a soft tall fescue into his ears. Ilham must have plugged it from the nearby bushes. "My friend, I noticed your interest in observing the movements of master Sam. But you need to be patient. You'll eventually have that opportunity, when the time comes," said Ilham while pulling Dhol away from the shaded area and walking a bit facing the crop plantation.

Ilham began, while pointing to the mountain, "Let me share with you about that peak. Adam's footprint is a "sacred footprint." It is a rock formation that shaped like a man's foot, placed near the summit. It is surrounded largely by forested hills, and with no mountain of comparable size nearby. You should remember well of your experience with the panther, as the mountain is a wildlife reserve, housing many species varying from elephants to leopards, and including many endemic species."

"The Peak is also very importantly located as a watershed. The lower areas benefited with good water flow for various agricultural activities." Ilham added with pride, sharing the good knowledge of his countryside.

"The districts to the south and the east of Adam's Peak produces various precious stones. You named any stones there are, and we have them here. This island is made famous of its Emeralds, rubies and sapphires," he continued.

The two men enjoyed the sceneries and its cooling breezes across the hilly area. More and more Dhol felt he missed home and the desire to complete his mission to search for his father and twin brother. But patience is needed for he has now added a new target along the way in achieving his goals.

As they approached the end of their third month there, the guards informed the prisoners to stop planting new seeds and veggies. According to one of the riders, master Sam believes he has done enough prayers of repentance there but appears to have lost hope that he will never ever get to sleep well again. Coupled with the peak pilgrimage season coming up, master Sam has decided to begin his journey to Mecca. Hence, all food supplies, along with their tents and newly bred cattle, were to be brought for the journey ahead.

"We have a week to go. I heard master Sam wants his daily bedtime stories to be told. Are you ready?" asked Kamil to Noah. "Master Sam will choose to hear from someone from a random tent each night." Suddenly Dhol felt suffocated. He can't imagine what would happen to him if his narration is not to the liking of master Sam......

Dub Dub Dub Dub. The sound grew louder with every footstep.

Chapter 9 - Water

The night and time have now arrived. Worst fears for all. Either you share a good story or ....be prepared to face the chopping block.

Dhol and his comrades turned out to be the first of the many to relate their knowledge to Master Sam. It was only until now, through Karl, who Dhol initially thought was chief of the guards, apparently is the advisor to master Sam, and closest aide-de-camp. And that Dhol realized that master Sam did not pick up just about anybody to follow his entourage. He screened their abilities, origins, competencies. Dhol remembered when he was first encountered by the guards alongside the beach, they spotted his ability to speak in multiple languages. And that with Malacca as a strategic city of trade, Dhol may be of good use to master Sam. Likewise, his other cell members, Kamil the historian of Al Andalus, Noah of Armenia whom has aplenty to relate of great prophets such as Prophet Noah. Ilham, on the other hand, may be useful for survival throughout their journey across Serendip and India.

Question is, who among them is to go first? Only master Sam will decide.

Karl and the guards approach their cell, bringing along with him a stack of new clothes. A box about the size of his fist was tossed to Dhol. "A soap box to make you and your friends smell good. A gift from master Sam. Make sure you shower and rub this soap all over your body and your hair." Dhol sniffed the box. Indeed, it smelled truly good. He has never experienced taking shower with soap before. Kamil cleared his throat and said with pride," I don't suppose that any of you know that the soap was invented by the scientists of Al Andalusia?" . "And there was where I originated. I therefore take pride and volunteer to be the first to share my story tonight." Everyone sighed as a sign of relief, to the least for now.

The prisoners' chains were removed. All smiles for their releases, but death awaits should any stories of none worthiness.

Kamil was the first to get ready. He seemed very eager to meet master Sam, and least to worry of possible backlash.

The men, accompanied by the guards, arrived at the big white tent. From far, the top of the tent had a shape of a button mushroom like. It took some 500 feet walk from their cell to master Sam's. The moon shared its light for the men's way towards the tent.

Master Sam, looking very composed, was seated on a half a knee height platform. The Persian red carpet and white sheep fur made the flooring looking majestic. A small carved mahagony wooden table in front of him had all the tropical fruits likened by the king. Master Sam was surrounded by colourful pillows wrapped in satins.

But a strange and noticeable difference about master Sam was that he had put up a mask, covering his eyes and nose. A black and gold coloured masquerade mask, if it fits more so. Dhol remembered that he had seen such mask before in one of the events held by the Portuguese celebration back home. The men hustled at each other, but the guards quickly pushed them to the floor heading area facing the back of master Sam.

Karl walked closer to master Sam, kneeled a bit and whispered to the master. It was not clear to anyone, but guessing logically, was to inform the presence of the prisoners into his master's tent. Karl then signalled to the men to decide who wishes to start his story telling.

Noah elbowed Kamil for he had agreed to be the spoke person for the night. Kamil quickly raised both hands, recites short do'a in haste. He then began," Dear master Sam. As per your wish, we have gathered here tonight to share our knowledge, experiences and exposures. All 4 of us came from different backgrounds and regions. I have volunteered to be the first person to relay my story. It is our hope that our little narration would benefit you from whichever way that is possible."

"Born and raised in Cordoba, I grew up in a city where knowledge and education are of prime. Cordoba is the center of research and discoveries. People from all over the world go there to tap the new findings, and make life better for their future generations. I have travelled far, and read many interesting facts," Kamil continued.

"But tonight, I wish to share with you the research and findings of an interesting gift from my Al Mighty Allah to the world. "

At this juncture, a husky voice was heard murmuring and interjecting Kamil's. It was not clear what he was saying. Everyone looked at each other, wondering where it came from. They didn't recognize the voice. But wait, it sounded like coming from Master Sam. Just a bit echoed. Perhaps due to the mask he was wearing.

Karl hurried to approach his master, listened for a while, nodded, then faced the men. "Among you men, one to be appointed as copywriter who will record these narrations. Master Sam wants the knowledge be kept well and shared with others and generations after." Karl add on," Dhol," looking sharp at Dhol and pointing to him to move to a small table at left corner of the tent. The table has several pieces of Chinese plain paper and quill pens placed on it. Dhol has seen and use some of those recently back home. As Malacca is a major trading port for Chinese merchants, Dhol helped his uncle with some trading engagements documents when he is not out for fishing.

Dhol hastily move to the table, but deep in his mind, wonder as to how did they know that he can write? Who could have told them? Dhol then remembered his small note book that he had brought along from home. He slipped his hand into his right pocket. But it was not there. Not in any of the other pockets. Not anywhere. Where had he left it? Dhol had no time to worry about this now. He will worry about the notebook later. For now, he needs to focus on the assignment vested on him. The block printing paper material given to work on are of new technology. The quill pen and ink truly attracted him. This is interesting. It might lead to something beneficial for Dhol and the rest of his newly found friends. Even for future generations to come.

Kamil cleared his throat. Perhaps hinting that he can't wait to start his story. " Water is, if not the most, at least one of the most important elements on earth. Every human that lives has more than half of his body filled with water. The earth has some form of water by more than half its area. Even human originated and created from a drop of sort of fluid as well. Not to forget all plants and trees and other living beings, all started with some form of water or fluid.

"You may wonder why I chose this topic as the first? The answer is simple. This is the very first element that our AL-Mighty Creator used to make out of us.

I read to you these 2 verses from our Holy Quran: "

Al Quran Surah At Tariq 86:5-6

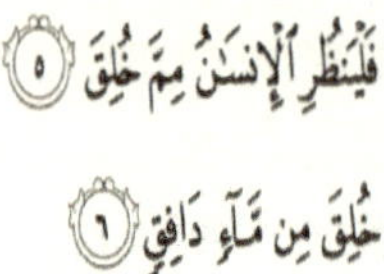

"So, let man observe from what he was created. He was created from a fluid, ejected...."

"You may wonder why I chose this topic as the first? The answer is simple. This is the very first element that was used to help create man. This is also the very first element that assist to bring the world to life

Al Quran Surah Al Fathir 35:27

"Do you not see that Allah sends down rain from the sky, and We produce thereby fruits of varying colours? And in the mountains are tracts, white and red of varying shades and [some] extremely black...."

"In addition, water is said to be influenced as to what is being recited by human. Scientists discovered that each verse of Quran, when recited to the water, will change the formation of its shape despite still having same composition. Scientists have tested it for several years and found that when we recite "Bismillah" before drinking regular water, quality of water improves for best drinking.

 "Reciting the 99 names of Allah produced a uniquely shaped form in the water composition that can help to heal various diseases and sickness. Take for example the name "Al Ghaffar" meaning "The Repeatedly Forgiving". If we continue reciting that name repetitively towards water before drinking it, we will eventually have a character of an individual who is forgiving. And I pray that all our hearts be softened and forgiving to one another and to the rest of others."

"When I was small, I always wonder why my older generations would recite verses of Quran having water in containers in front of them. They then would ask children to drink those water as daily consumption." At this juncture, Master Sam nodded and interjected. "That is very true. Especially when we were sick or having troubles, discomfort, or even worries."

To that, Kamil smiled while nodded in agreement. There seemed to have interaction with Master Sam. A good sign. He is human after all.

 "Hence, Master Sam. The fact that you have every intention to travel to Mecca, and that we are to follow, it is even more benefiting for you to know that ZamZam, the water that is only available there, is even said to be a miracle." Kamil continued with the rest showing deep interest to the subject. "This ZamZam has the quality of the highest grade that no other water in this world has. Zamzam in Mecca is no ordinary water. Scientists discovered that when Zamzam water is diluted, regardless of multiple times, it is not affected of its quality. Quite reversely, one drop of Zamzam water, when mixed with 1000 drops of any regular water, will result to the regular water changing its form and produces the same quality as ZamZam water. It is that pure that of no equivalence elsewhere on this earth."

 "Water, just as similar to human, reacts either positively or negatively to its surroundings. This liquid, may form itself into various types of crystal-like shapes depending on the words, recitations, prayers, and feelings of its surrounding human. "

Dhol, at this point, raised his hands, signaled to Kamil as if he was requesting for a time out. Dhol needed to ensure he wrote it all and not missed any important facts.

As Dhol was back to his speed, he gave a thumbs up to Kamil to continue his narration. "Scientists also have proven that, the Muslim practice recitation of BISMILLAH before eating and drinking on any regular water, will produce a positive change in formation to the structure of water particles, making the best out of it for our body system and health. This is very much aligned with the practice of our forefathers, where, if someone recites the Quran on regular water, it gets the ability for the treatment of different diseases."

"My little but hopefully beneficial advice to you Master Sam, is to find the right Asma ul Husna of Allah and start reciting it consistently throughout your days ahead, to the water you intend to drink. And keep saying prayers for Allah is forever and always most forgiving. May you heal and fulfil your wishes from whatever you wish for." Ended Kamil on his night of sharing.

"Subhan'Allah!" said master Sam, to everyone's surprise. "Surely this is a Miracle of Allah's," he added. " This strengthens my desire to visit Mecca, which I am planning to do soon." All in the room was dead silent. None said a word, but nodded in agreement of his intention.

The men walked back to their cell with heads held high, full or satisfaction. The fears they had thought all along of being executed has changed completely. It felt like a new beginning, new life, exciting days ahead. More knowledge for all.

Somehow, the men sat among themselves and pondered again what had just happened. What exactly was in master Sam's mind? What would happen to them in coming days? How long is this story narration thingy to continue? When will each of them be released and pursue their respective goals in life?

There was a moment of silence. Then Dhol threw a suggestion," I saw good in what we just did. I visualized stars in our future. I am willing to delay my pursuit of searching my loved ones for a good cause. Umi, my late mom will be proud of what I'm doing. We may end up gaining much more than we ever thought of," which unanimously were accepted by all. "From tonight onwards, let us strategize our narration, topics, knowledge sharing. We can make a book out of this. We share to the world. Spread it out. May our efforts not only for master Sam's recovery, but way beyond generations." To that, the prisoners put their hands together as solidarity of brotherhood.

As the rest dozed off, Dhol performed a short prayer. He flipped a verse from the Holy Quran, taken from chapter Luqman 31:27 and ponder upon the meaning of these verses. He looked up to the sky and whisper of thanks for all that he gone through for the day. No human could ever come close to invent, or even copy the tiniest of creatures that The Al-Mighty had given its inventions to enjoy on this universe.

وَلَوْ أَنَّمَا فِى ٱلْأَرْضِ مِن شَجَرَةٍ أَقْلَـٰمٌ وَٱلْبَحْرُ يَمُدُّهُۥ مِنۢ بَعْدِهِۦ سَبْعَةُ أَبْحُرٍ مَّا نَفِدَتْ كَلِمَـٰتُ ٱللَّهِ إِنَّ ٱللَّهَ عَزِيزٌ حَكِيمٌ ۝

"And if all the trees on earth were pens and the ocean [were ink], with seven oceans behind it to add to its [supply], yet would not the words of

Allah be exhausted [in the writing]: for Allah is Exalted in Power, full of Wisdom."

Al Fussilat 41:53 which read:

سَنُرِيهِمْ ءَايَٰتِنَا فِى ٱلْءَافَاقِ وَفِىٓ أَنفُسِهِمْ حَتَّىٰ يَتَبَيَّنَ لَهُمْ أَنَّهُ ٱلْحَقُّ أَوَلَمْ يَكْفِ بِرَبِّكَ أَنَّهُۥ عَلَىٰ كُلِّ شَىْءٍ شَهِيدٌ ۝

"We will show them Our signs in the horizons and within themselves until it becomes clear to them that it is the truth. But is it not sufficient concerning your Lord that He is, over all things, a Witness?"

Chapter 10 - Anticlockwise

That morning never felt better for Dhol, or for anyone in the cell for that matter. A new lease of life. They may not have managed to help master Sam to get to sleep, yet a fresh new perspective of his interests and expectations. " Hey, Pheewwiitt," Dhol whistled to a guard that passed by their cell. " Can you inform Karl to have more Chinese milled papers in master Sam's tent for tonight? We have a lot to write and I don't want it to affect the flow of narrations," Dhol explained. The guard nodded, then left without saying a word. Dhol also intend to request master Sam to delay his travel to Mecca a little longer as he believes that they were just beginning to establish a good momentum on their story nights.

That night arrived. Kamil is not done just yet. He has many more to share. As it is dusk, it gets tougher for them to see the path, but as they were making their way to master Sam's, Kamil said to the rest, " I'm continuing my story for the night. The least, you gentlemen will have more time to prepare and beef up your

contents before the turn of your actual days,".
Noah tapped Kamil's shoulder and whispered.
They handshake and continued walking to join
the other 2, whom had almost reached the big
mushroom tent.

At the large center area of the tent, the men
waited anxiously for Dhol to signal that he was
ready to record the story of the night. Dhol
supposed his message to Karl earlier today got
through. A pile of Chinese milled papers was
well stacked close to where he was expected to
be seated. As he dipped the quill pen into the
ink can, he then smiled to Kamil, indicating that
he is ready. Noah and Ilham were seated side by
side, right behind Kamil. Ilham sat resting on
both his heels. Noah sat on his left foot along
the ground with the right foot upright. Those
were the positions they are used to when
performing their daily prayers. The Master,
expressionless behind his mask on just like the
night before, observed well of the men in
presence.

Kamil turned to Noah, who is eager to take the lead. They hurriedly switch sitting places. Noah started with gesturing his brothers to raise both hands as a sign of do'a. He then recited,"

اللَّهُمَّ إِنِّي أَسْأَلُكَ عِلْمًا نَافِعًا

"O Allah, I ask You for knowledge that is of benefit,"

وَرِزْقًا طَيِّبًا وَعَمَلاً مُتَقَبَّلاً

" A good provision, and deed that will be accepted."

"Aamiin," followed by all. Master Sam somehow, lowered his face looking to the floor, with both hands covering it. He stayed at that position for a while. And a little longer. It was quite apparent that there were secrets behind the mask that only he knew. The men waited for him to lift his face before they proceed with the next chapter of narration. Noah's recitation of prayer may be short, but it could have had a deep meaning and touched master Sam that had the master pausing for thoughts. But Noah does not intend to allow a change in any of the men's focus of the night.

He instead began," As I see it, there are many reasons for doing specific actions. Some with simple logic, some requires more in-depth research and knowledge. For generations, it has been the rituals of Muslims to perform circumambulation known as "Tawaaf" around the Kaaba. Be it for the spiritual aspects, mental, physical or any matters, the Kaaba had never stopped being circum-ambulated by humans. Not to anyone's knowledge that any single moment of time that Kaaba is empty from being tawaaf, ever since it was re-built by Prophet Abraham. Thou it was first built by Adam, perhaps there was a period during the great flood in the era of Prophet Noah's ice age that no praise momentarily to AlMighty Allah was conducted in such act due to the flood."

"Question is, why was this particular "walking around in circular motion ritual" done in anticlockwise circulation?" , Noah asked. "But before I go on further, I must take this opportunity to share and explain what it means of anticlockwise. Somewhere in England in 13th century, the English invented clock. A clock is a machine invented to measure time. Mankind had evolved from the time where we use stones and sticks to gauge dawn, midday, and dusk. The English invented the first clock and the German, later in 15th century, improvised it into a smaller size version named watch, portable, and they can carry it with them wherever they go, tied it to their hands or keep in their pockets. "

 "Now, this clock or watch are using a mechanism that measure the movement of day based on the sun. The inventors uses sundials, believing that the sun appears to move across the sky in a clockwise direction. This was how the term originated. As for other worldly orders, movements are anticlockwise." Noah continues.

 "With that concept in mind, I want to bring you back to our main story of Tawaaf at Kaaba in anticlockwise."

 Noah then stood up, walked a few steps to the front heading towards master Sam. Midway, he stopped at the table and grabbed a black cubic like shaped box and placed it in the center of his left hand, [apparently used by master Sam as a weight to hold small papers from flying when blown by wind]. It was of a size smaller than his palm. Noah then raised his right hand just slightly on top of the black cube, but leaving only his thumb pointing upwards. He then explained," Look everyone, let's just imagine that this black cube is the Kaaba. And my right hand that is clasply gripped with the right thumb pointing upwards as circular motion surrounding Kaaba. You'll noticed that all fingers are in the similar direction from left to right. If we look at it from top, it is of circular motion moving in anticlockwise. " You see, the continuous movements in same direction anticlockwise will create waves. These waves will become a force as it gets stronger. And that it will move upwards via the thumb. Up, up and away. "

 "Visualize this further. Muslims all over the world, regardless wherever they are, pray towards the same direction, facing the Kaaba. And those that are praying and performing the tawaaf will keep circum-ambulating around it. Humans continue to ask for forgiveness, good health, safety, wealth, longer life, success, and all sorts of demands, at every single second in different time zones throughput the day. These doa's and prayers keeps coming and circling around, and eventually move upwards. This creates currents of electromagnets, sending them across the sky and above. It symbolically addresses to Allah a unified request from His servants to the Creator. And knowing Allah as being The Most Gracious, The Most Merciful, it touches His heart to hear all the prayers signifying how much His servants remember Him. And by His Grace, our wishes are granted."

"Science has also discovered many things that mapped the logic of several important life practicalities, and they are of no coincidences. The studies of medicine discover that Blood inside the human body begins its circulation "Anticlockwise". The scientists found out that electrons of an atom revolve around its nucleus in the same manner as making Tawaf, in an anti-clockwise direction. The physicists noted that the moon revolves around the earth anti-clockwise. Even the earth rotates around its own axis in an anti-clockwise direction. They later realized that earth revolves around the sun, also, in an anti-clockwise direction. As human discoveries progress, the astronomists came across their findings that the planets of the Solar system revolve around the sun in an anti-clockwise direction. They then came to know the Sun along with its whole Solar system orbit in the galaxy in an anti-clockwise direction. Perhaps, some day in the future, scientists may also realize that all the galaxies may be orbiting in the space in an anti-clockwise direction."

" In conclusion, when we revolve around the Kaaba we are orbiting in the same direction as the whole universe. Worshipping Allah in one direction. Praising Allah in one direction. And all these creations of Allah, right from the tiniest particles, to the largest galaxies, along with the human race unite in praise of Allah. All in same direction".

"Science made these discoveries from time to time, bit by bit. More discoveries are likely in years and time to come. Humans are astonished by these findings. But we forgot that our Al Mighty creator had all along instructed us to stay synchronized with the rest of His creations to attain the best in all executions. The tawaaf is a very simple real-life example. But we didn't take note that such revelations and commandments had been assigned to us ever since the beginning of mankind's existence. Our forefather, Adam, was tasked to set the foundation of Kaaba. Abraham, re-built the very same monument after the great flood. Prophet Muhammad, perfected the cracked portion of the Aswad edge. They all perform the tawaaf around the Kaaba anticlockwise."

"I share these discoveries with you, not to show that I am smarter and better off than you. I did this to remind me of the many rituals I have been practising for tens of years, but very little performed with conscientiousness, with clear understanding of why I did them, what are the rational, significance, benefits that I will get. I share with you with the hope that together, we understand the fundamentals, hence spread out the knowledge to the rest, be it during this era, as well as for the future generations."

"Our great prophets sacrificed so much throughout their lives that they dedicated their works for the good of human. I am so blessed to be born, raised, and educated in the land where prophet Noah landed his ark. An ark of such size that no average man could build without first having in-depth knowledge on architecture, engineering, and navigation. An ark that has the quality to withstand the hardest blows of the sea, using material that lasted over tens of thousands of years. Having travelled half the globe, I visited sites of great cities of previous civilizations and witness how successful those generations had been. From humble beginnings, the kings build empires and rose to stardom, filled with wealth, power, and conquest. Sadly, greed and arrogance led them to self-destructions."

Ar Ruum 30:9

أَوَلَمْ يَسِيرُوا۟ فِى ٱلْأَرْضِ فَيَنظُرُوا۟ كَيْفَ كَانَ عَٰقِبَةُ ٱلَّذِينَ مِن قَبْلِهِمْ ۚ كَانُوٓا۟ أَشَدَّ مِنْهُمْ قُوَّةً وَأَثَارُوا۟ ٱلْأَرْضَ وَعَمَرُوهَآ أَكْثَرَ مِمَّا عَمَرُوهَا وَجَآءَتْهُمْ رُسُلُهُم بِٱلْبَيِّنَٰتِ ۖ فَمَا كَانَ ٱللَّهُ لِيَظْلِمَهُمْ وَلَٰكِن كَانُوٓا۟ أَنفُسَهُمْ يَظْلِمُونَ ﴿٩﴾

"Have they not travelled through the earth and observed how was the end of those before them? They were greater than them in power, and plowed the earth and built it up more than they have built it up, and their messengers came to them with clear evidences. And Allah would not ever wronged them, but they were wronging themselves."

The tent was the only bright spot around the base of Adam's Peak. Perhaps the night was filled with Baroqah and wisdom brought down for the men from above. Aamiin.

Chapter 11 – Story of two men

The day drew faster than it used to. At least that's how it felt for the prisoners. None of them woke up for the Subuh prayer. It was a sound of chain lock for the cell being removed that woke Ilham. The rest were still sound asleep.

"Good, the right person that I need to see. As a gesture of thanks, Master Sam wants you and your colleagues to take a rest from sharing stories of your own. He instead wants you, Ilham, to be the narrator for tonight. But you are lucky. All you need to do is read from this book and share for all to hear," the guard tossed the book to Ilham. The guard was about to lock the cell when Ilham shakenly replied," Wait, I don't know how to read and write." To that, the guard smiled," That's your problem. Be prepared to face the consequence.......hahaha" and he left.

Ilham got so petrified, that he peed instantly. He then fell flat on Noah's tummy, who was still asleep next to him. The fall woke everyone. The

men quickly sprinkled some water to wake
Ilham up, conscious. They had a small pouch of
water from master Sam's tent that Ilham had
taken slickly from last night.

New problem. They have to figure a way to
save a friend from any possibilities. How????

The night came. The men had cleansed
themselves and put on newly washed clothes
provided by their master. They seemed calm
and ready. Not with faces of troubles. Not even
Ilham. Dhol clutches Ilham's shoulder with tight
grip, giving him the warmth, from a big brother.
Together they walk with confidence heading to
the very same mushroom head like tent.

As they arrive, master Sam was as usual seated
with his back facing the men. From the side, his
was still having his mask on to cover the identity
of the man that not one of the prisoners had
seen before.

Dhol took the lead to speak on behalf of the
group for this time. He asked to be rested from
writing the narration just for the day as the
story was only to be read from a book, which

was already been documented. To that, master Sam agreed. Dhol then sat right behind Ilham.

The men were fortunate to not have Karl and the guards around tonight. They heard that Karl and several guards were asked to go down the edge of the mountain to invite a famous scholar. This will take a few days.

Ilham then asked to begin. As the book is quite big, he raised the book high enough to cover his face from potentially being seen by master Sam. "ehem ehem," he cleared his throat. But his voice sounded slightly different. A bit huskier and deeper. The prisoners knew the trick, but hopefully not master Sam. And it was the voice of Dhol who recites as a cover up of Ilham. Kamil and Noah started making do'a quietly with the hope that the night will end smoothly without master Sam noticing Dhol's voice in replace of Ilham.

Then Ilham, as in Dhol, flipped to the first page and started his recitation:

Once there were twin brothers. They never truly met each other as they got split when they were very young. It was due to a war. They elder grew up with the mother. They younger escaped the nation along with the father for protection. The plan was for the father to return home and bring along his wife and other son. He never did return.

The twins grew up in different parts of the world. Despite the different exposures, locations, and methods of bringing up, they both turned up to become very smart and successful in life. They obviously were raised by different approaches and cultures. Yet acquired good business skills, language, communication, respect and perseverance, as well as spiritual and religious knowledge.

The elder of the twin lived a quiet and humble life. He was very well liked by people around him. He personalized a character of humility, personified maturity and leadership. But financially, suffice to sustain basic needs to support him and his mother. That was all that was known about him.

At this juncture, Dhol paused his reading for a while. This sounds familiar. It sounded like his story……. "Hmmm…Ah", just a coincidence, he said to his heart. He flipped to the next page and continued.

The younger brother worked very hard and grew his business empire of multiple activities.

He travelled to many parts of the world and expand his wealth by leaps and bounds. He met the rich and famous. He made a reputation via his engagements with many noble associates and elites.

Despite his success, he is very religious and charitable. He gave out alms, donated money and food to the poor, helped build shelters and financed some institutions to educate younger generations to learn read and write. He became known widely in the region though at a young age of 30s. He eventually was offered to marry the daughter of a wealthy merchant in a neighbouring country.

In a storyline like many others, he began to have rivalries and enemies. His business was sabotaged, his crops and farm were burnt, his calves and sheep poisoned, caravans stolen and many other incidents that had ever been done before. Yet he persevered and re-build his empire. This created even a lot more anger among his business competitors.

They began to pretend to be closest of his friends. They followed him everywhere. They praised him of his wealth and success, and treated him as if he was God. They tried to introduce him to liquor and shisha. They then bought in women for his pleasure. Their attempt continued for some time. To their surprise, he stood strong and never neglect his beautiful wife.

They strategized a final step. They must get rid of the wife. This could bring him down completely. Hence, just before his return in one of his business trips from abroad, they sent a young and handsome man into his mansion and sneaked into bed while his wife was asleep.

As it was late night upon his arrival, he decided to not disturb his wife. He tiptoed quietly in the dark into his room for he wanted to surprise her in case she woke up. As he sneaked into bed, the stranger was obviously in between him and the wife. This episode of the night was a complete disaster of his marriage. His anger shot to the sky. It was chaos. Shouts and screams and punches and kicks objects thrown all over was all that was.

He rushed to the left side table within his reach and grabbed a dagger. A dagger that he always carries within his belt. A dagger with blue and red jewels crowned at its head. And that was for customary, for style, for protection. The dagger was specially made with double edged and jagged on its outer side.

The stranger jumped out of bed naked. He was of fair skin, burly, with light thin beard. He struggled to search for his clothes scattered all over the floor.

The wife, who had slept soundly after taking her medication, was still groggy and confused with what was actually happening. She had no clue who the stranger was. Had the least idea that her husband had just arrived. No idea of the set up. She was petrified, later screamed aimlessly. She stood up but was a little high and drowsy. She held her forehead in disbelief of seeing what was happening in front of her eyes. The husband was slaughtered the stranger's neck with just one stroke. He slashed him with his dagger all over the stranger's body. Blood was splurging out of the stranger's body in every part.

Dhol had to pause reading. If he would have taken time to read the content prior to coming to Master Sam's tent, he wouldn't have agreed to replace Ilham this very night. This was such sadist. Unthinkable of. He never thought that it would be him to have come across and a reader of such a write up. At a moment where their gathering was meant to acquire knowledge and learnings.

Who wrote this book? Why on earth did Master Sam asked Ilham to read it? This is so puzzling. Dhol paused longer. But Ilham elbowed him to continue. A little concern that Master Sam might realize of their trick as replacement reader.

Master Sam interjected. "I am certain that you all have loads of questions circling around your head about the book." He quipped, then continue. "Let me end up the story myself as I truly well know every single second of that incident. You may close the book and I will take it from there."

"The man never stopped slashing the stranger until he was certain that the stranger was lifeless." The man subsequently turned to his wife and pulled her hair. She fell to the ground. He locked her body in between his legs. She was so stunt that she didn't know how to react and what to say. She was so confused. Besides, she was very sick and weak. The husband didn't wait long before skinning her face with the dagger, that he held firmly with his left hand. She struggled in pain but the husband never waited a moment to reconsider his act. He then slit her throat till her neck was almost displaced from her body.

There lied 2 lifeless bodies on the floor. A split second of unimaginable mishaps of the night.

"And that husband, that man, that killer, that was me." exclaimed Master Sam.

All in the room were stunned. It never crossed their mind of such tragic, horrendous act was Master Sam himself. A silent moment for a longer period that night. No one dared to look up at Master Sam's face. No one had any clue this was the closing chapter for the night.

"I will end here. And this story ends here as well. I will leave it to you draw your conclusion. But I have ears should the story spreads beyond this point You may leave to your shelter this instance," Said Master Sam.

That night felt like it went by faster. Each and every mate's heart beat a certain. Their plan to save Ilham worked. And they had done themselves proud by saving a friend's life. The trick worked. And it worked out very well. Another day is saved.

But they came across a lot more. A secret that they have wanted to know about. They have the answer now.

Each looked amongst themselves. But none dared to speak. For they may not see each other again. The night ended with more puzzling questions as for the ending.....

Chapter 12 - The Malacca Downfall

Today was the fourth day of story-telling nights. Kamil, Noah, and Ilham were done. Dhol, despite having read the book on Arm's behalf, cannot escape his turn. He has got to produce his part or no one knows what would happen to them. Their goals have shifted slightly, as in a delay in pursuing their individual objectives, with an add on initiatives. Initiatives that they believe will benefit many more.

Master Sam waited impatiently for Dhol to start his narration. Despite hiding his face behind the mask, it was very obvious that Master Sam was facing straight towards Dhol. The whole area grew dead silence that a drop of pin would break the nightly focus. Dhol began with his cracked, a little tremble shaken voice.

"My real name is Abdullah. I come from a family of the nobles. My grandfather was the former Interior Minister of the famous Malacca

Sultanate Kingdom and its Archipelago and ruling territories. It was during his service was when Malacca was attacked and fell to the hands of the Portuguese."

"My mother was more loved by the Al-Mighty and had returned to him a week before my departure here. I now travelled to fulfil my mother's wish in search of my long-lost father and my twin brother of some 30 years. I believe they are in Mecca, hence, my journey.

We were supposed to fled Malacca together when the war erupted. A huge Portuguese cannon came pounding and blasted right on the shore where our tug boat was about to leave for the large vessel. My father managed to arrive onto the ship with my twin brother in time before the invaders' arrival. He was supposed to return for us after putting my twin brother safely on board the ship that day. But the Portuguese got closer. We couldn't escape. My uncle, PakSu, was in the boat behind us. He had to make up stories that we were foreigners, to save us from being further questioned. My mother, sadly, fainted from the loud bomb blast. I was in her arms crying, but well protected in a sarong and wrapped around her chest. All this was told and repeated over by my mother as I grew up."

"Back in Malacca later on, we lived in a modest remote village house to the south of the city in disguise hailing from neighbouring state of Perak. We changed our names and cut ties with the palace. All as per instructions from my grandfather who fled the city along with the Sultan to the south. "

At this juncture, Master Sam was noticed to have pulled a cloth from his right pocket into his mask to wipe his face. Dhol would have guess that Master Sam was wiping his tears. But why would it be for? Perhaps some dust may have caught into his eyes. The friends seemed focus and impatient for Dhol to continue.

"I have every intention to share about the downfall of Malacca as I want the generations after us to have some insight of some parts of the overall downfall. And that history will help us to rise and bring back the glory of our forefathers. Now that you want us to record these stories, this is an opportunity for me to contribute for the benefit of future civilizations and lessons learned from it."

Dhol continued.

" The Kingdom of Malacca lies within the Malay Archipelago. Malacca Kingdom stretches way up in north from the southern islands of Mindanao, to the south eastern islands of Makassar. On the west, it covers the territories of Indo-China, southern Siam, the whole of Malay Peninsular, till the south of sea of Sumatera. Temasek, in the south-island, ends the kingdom reigns.

 This story was narrated to me by my uncle, who was told of the same by my grandfather. My grandfather was the Interior Minister of Malacca during the fall of our great nation to the hands of the Portuguese in 1511 AD. A scenario where while Portuguese forces surrounded the last fort and castle of the Malaccan Sultanate, a political struggle rages within, as those aligned with influential ministers, the interior and foreign, in attempts to sway their leader in his response to the Portuguese invaders.

 'My narration is verbatim of the same from my uncle and from my grandfather, hence with some conversations between several of the Sultan that I recall, explained Dhol on how the flow of his story for the night. Master Sam seemed to node his head from the movements seen despite his face is behind his mask.

Dhol began, "Your Tuanku Sultan, the Minister of Interior has arrived from south of the city," informed her consort to Sultan Mansur Shah, the Sultan of Malacca". The Sultan coughed several times, to which the palace maid quickly pulled a small metal bin for him to spit his phlegm into. She then wiped the Sultan's saliva from the sides of his mouth with a gold coloured handkerchief.

Sultan Mansur walked to his throne in the main reception hall with all ministers bowing down as a show of respect. "Does the enemy truly talk of a peace treaty?" Sultan asked. "The Portuguese Admiral Alfonso d'Alburqurque demands to know why the Malaccans broke the promise of brotherhood," informed Interior Minister. "Portuguese has no intention of waging war, only seeks to renew the pledge," he added. The Sultan asked," Any signs of follow-up forces?". To that, the Minister replied," None, except for the spearhead forces led by vice Admiral". "You are so naïve, Interior Minister, to believe the white people!" interjected by Prime Minister. Interior Minister then responded," I can only tell you what I witnessed at the enemy camp." Prime Minister then asked," And what are the conditions for the peace treaty?". The Sultan then further asked," Do they wish for us to terminate our business dealings with the middle east?" Interior Minister replied," Your Tuanku Sultan, I'm obliged to inform you that the condition is to have you to pay a visit to the Portuguese battle ship Flor d'Lamar. And seek apology on behalf of you and the kingdom of Malacca."

Meanwhile, inside the battleship, advisor to Alfonso posed the question," Will the Malaccans meet our demands?". Alfonso smiled as replied," They are narrow-minded enough to put moral obligations first." I don't expect they will give in easily,". "What are their alternatives, then?". "They will buy themselves time to think of a way out." the advisor replied. "And if we give them the time they seek, will they succeed?" asked Alfonso more. "Why are Malaccan people so foolish?" to that the advisor said," The mountain is steep, and fortress looks solid. But the Malaccan's walls are flimsy. Once the wooden fences are completed, block all paths in and out of the fortress. We bombard them with our latest technology missiles until the walls collapse. They do not have weaponry as advanced as we do."

In the palace, the emergency meeting continued. "There will not be any peace treaty," informed the Interior Minister. " Your Tuanku

Sultan, regretfully, I must tell you, if we fail to negotiate a peace treaty now, we will face the wrath of the barbaric Portuguese.....". " Foreign Minister continued, "The enemy has travelled a long way. They are exhausted. Put a bounty on their heads." To that, Interior Minister responded," Are we serving the country by using swords in place of words? It is not death I fear, but the future of the country is at stake."

The Sultan has heard enough of his ministers' views. "You may leave now, all of you," as he coughed when leaving the courtroom.

....

....

Much to Dhol's surprise, master Sam snored and was heard by all in the bedroom. This is, for the first time, master Sam fell asleep during the story telling nights.

Dhol and everyone in the room left quietly with a great relief.

Dhol flipped through some verses from The Holy Book. He reflected the rest Master Sam needed that was so long overdue and found The

Al-Mighty's revelation. It was so spot on for human natural needs and he couldn't agree more.

Al Quran chapter An Naba' 78: 7-8

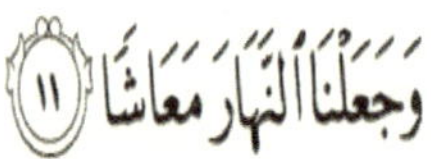

"And [He] made the night as clothing [resting]"

"And [He] made the day for livelihood."

Chapter 13 - Insomnia No More

Master Sam jolted from his sleep. The day was as bright as mid day. It was indeed mid-day! "Did I fall asleep this long? Did I? Did I?" Master Sam couldn't believe himself that he had had a long night of dose. He stood up feeling joy, satisfied, as if like in heaven. He smiled, feeling overjoyed and then recalled, it wasn't Dhol who made this happened. His story wasn't that great that got me to sleep so soundly. Could it be that it was that boring that had caused it? But something about Dhol that made him feel good. Comfortable. Warm. Stable. Could it be the one that he was told about long ago? But for now, let's not get carried away with too many things on his mind. "Karl, bring me the Malaccan boy and his friends," master Sam instructed.

The guards came along with Dhol and the other 3 prisoners a while later. "Sir, the prisoners as your command," said the burly guard having pushed the men to the floor facing master Sam. 'Listen, from today, I want these men be given good food, cleansed, new clothes. Tonight, Dhol must continue about Malacca from where he stopped last night. And to you, Dhol, I demand that even if you are done with your Malacca fables, you are to be present here every night there is to be until we reach Mecca. I regard you as god's gift and a sign that my prayers are answered and that these initiatives of story-telling material that we began to document, will flourish and be used to the good of mankind. Secure them well, and bring it along wherever we go to be shared as knowledge on history, science, religion, politics, and most of all AlMighty's scriptures for the benefit of all coming generations of human."

Master Sam added, "And release all other prisoners immediately. They are free to go wherever they want. I have found the right people I need," while looking at Dhol and friends. It was difficult to guess how master Sam's facial expression looked like from behind his mask. But his intonation alone is sufficient to signal a voice of positivity, delight, joy, happy, thankful.

The prisoners looked at each other, eyes glowed, all smiles. Never would Dhol imagined that his story has helped master Sam to gain his sleep again. Dhol's eyes got watery. Tears of joy. Tears of thankful to the AlMighty, for He has given a chance for Dhol to make good to another creation of His. "Syukran ya Allah, subhanallah".

Ilham too smiled at him as they walk back to their camp. "You saved our lives. I must thank you for what you did." Kamil and Noah pat Dhol's shoulders for a job well done.

....
....

That night, after Isyak prayer and dinner, Dhol and his friends walk freely and joyfully to master Sam's place. Several other guards were on standby in the tent as master Sam just concluded his prayers recitation. They waited to be seated on the furry sheep carpet, around his velvet sheet platform, located at the corner of the room with some drinks and fruits already placed in front of them on a small but neatly arranged wooden side table. This is in contrast to all previous nights where they were greeted without carpets, drinks, food, new clothes, poker faces, sword holding to the throat like reception.

Dhol continued his story. "The night was getting a bit colder after a heavy rain earlier the day. Interior Minister and Admiral was walking uphill around the walls of the fortress to survey its condition and the state of their soldiers. " How many soldiers are in the fortress now?" asked Interior Minister. "Including those at the fortress under my command, the local soldiers from the nearby provinces, and the men from the village, we have a total of 6,000." " I understand that the enemy's number is half of that, but with more superior weapons and advanced machineries," sigh Interior Minister. " This fortress was built on a natural barrier. My fear was that the continuous rain for the past one month could weaken the foundations. The Portuguese bombs and cannons are very modern and powerful. This coupled with hunger, children and women that will break our spirit even before the enemy physically reaches us," said Admiral.

Back at one of the houses within the fortress, Interior Minister was later called by the Sultan for a one on one discussion. The Sultan inquired, "Supposedly I do not go, what would most likely, you think. They're reaction?" In which Interior Minister replied. "They will then gather their forces. Highly likely that they will breach the fortress walls."

"Is this their idea, or yours?" raised the Sultan twice to the Interior Minister. " It is what their

interpreter told me. He sits alongside Alfonso." "
But I just cannot go. I'd rather die a slave than
surrendering. "With your permission, Your
Tuanku Sultan, I must leave for the battleship
this instance. We need to negotiate before they
lose their patience." said Interior Minister. The
Sultan asks further, "Do you think there is a
chance of negotiation?" he replied," Your
Tuanku Sultan, I would rather die facing the
enemy's sword, instead of lingering here a
second longer."

The Sultan continues," But I hear the fortress is
surrounded." The Interior Minister replied," Do
not worry, Your Tuanku Sultan. I will find a way,
at all cost." He asked for permission to arrange
for another round of negotiation with the
enemy. And he then left.

Dhol was about to continue his story when
master Sam's snore, again caught everyone's
attention. The men rolled their eyes towards
the fruit basket at the corner table. They quietly
but swiftly adjourn and fill their arms and
clothes with all the food and fruits en-route to
their cell. A second straight day of sleep for the
insomniac master Sam. Indeed, a blessed night
again for the prisoners.

Chapter 14 - The Deal is off

"At dawn, the next morning, Interior Minister left quietly on his brown horse from the fortress heading towards southeast Malacca Port. He brought along with him a knee high dowry tree made from gold, firmly wrapped in a silk batik, covered in a rectangular velvet case. He carried it as a bag-pack strapped onto his shoulder. He reached the entry point by midday, leading him to be given an ambassador welcome by the Portuguese infantry. Along his way from the fortress, the enemy army is seen everywhere preparing long ladders made from wooden bamboos. It is so obvious that they are meant be used to climb the fortress. Food supply are abundance for the army. Military artilleries and huge cannons are being deployed for designated stations for the bombardment. He compared with the state the fortress is in, he sensed that with one attack, Malacca is doom for destruction. "

"Within the fortress' walls, they are rationing food supply, with limited guns and powders of previous generation, traditional military equipment of bows and arrows. Interior minister can't help but cried in his heart, thinking the fate of his nation in coming days."

"As he arrived at the main entrance, the interpreter greeted him with announcement by the entrance captain," Admiral Alfonso welcomes Interior Minister as an Ambassador of Malacca." they both walked into the boat to be taken to the battleship. This is the third visit he made in two weeks. He prayed that it will not be the last and final, for the sake of the nation. Malacca is known for its expertise in negotiations, both on war and business. But of late, trust and respect became the most fragile form of surrender that exist there. The Sultan's mercurial decisions has created many disagreements and chaos among the trading nations. His ministers' interferences and disagreements among them had caused many factions and are not helping at all. Above all, it is his weakness and inability to administer is paramount to the fall of the nation.

Interior Minister waited to be seated as they arrived at the upper deck of the ship. A room with chandelier and leather sofa may not look appropriate for a battle ship, as a sign of luxury the Portuguese has in their status. But his nation is at stake, and that must take priority.

His focus must be for the nation. If Malacca wins the battle, status and pride will be restored.

A tall late fifties Caucasian man holding a pipe walked into the room. "Your excellency" greeted the man. "Admiral" replied Interior Minister with a deep low voice in response. The Interior Minister then firmly but steadily push forward the case he brought with him after untying the knot. Glows of gold brightened the room, coming from the case. "Gift from the Sultan." Alfonso's faced turned red. " The Portuguese King has been generous in having sparred your life so far. And in not yet destroying the fortress." Alfonso said in anger. Yet he paused, then helped pour a cup of coffee to the acceptance of the Minister. Alfonso then continued," Your face has grown thin and gaunt." In reply, the Minister said," I appreciate your concern. But I seek your counsel's consideration to review your request for the Sultan's presence here." Alfonso responded," I have already told you what I want. Do you prefer to start a war with that little wall between us?" as Alfonso grab a rifle on his left while inserting a bullet into it. "I am very certain that there must be another way," replied the Interior Minister. Alfonso's voice got deeper," It is your Sultan's fault we are where we find ourselves today. The King seeks justice by punishing your Sultan." " This is not his fault, but more to the subject." replied Interior Minister. "I myself would accept whatever punishment I am due," he added with a bit shaken voice, as having the rifle pointed at him from point blank.

Interior Minister knew there is not much more that he can negotiate as the Portuguese reached their limit of patience. "What sort of punishment would you prefer? Are you willing to give your life?" Alfonso asked. With due respect, the Interior Minister has earned the praised from Alfonso for upholding his wisdom in handling the negotiation when he replied," If my life would open a path of peace, then....". Alfonso swayed to the window and pulled the trigger, shooting blindly across the straits open air instead. "Bring the Sultan. No other option. And in a weeks' time. Else you know what is coming," ordered Alfonso.

The Interior Minister paddled his horse as fast as he could, back to the fortress knowing that time is not on the Malaccan side. It was at dusk as he reached the palace ground, when he heard calls from the council of ministers from outside the palace entrance," Your Tuanku Sultan, Interior Minister was sent to the enemy's camp to beg for our lives. Such an act disgraces Your Tuanku Sultan! Even in the times of peace, there is always a traitor. But none like Interior Minister, who has thrown the Sultan to the enemy! Everyone within the fortress call him 'son of Alfonso'. Have him executed, You Tuanku Sultan. We will fight the Portuguese till the end."

A sovereign state it used to be, highly respected and looked up to by the region, Malacca used to be the icon of an Islamic model nation, even by the likes of China. The Chinese Emperor during the Ming Dynasty had sent his princess, Hang Li Po to be married to the powerful Sultan Mansur Shah, as a sign acknowledging the importance of Malacca to the Chinese empire.

With the Straits of Malacca as the main passage between Europe and the east, Malacca became the busiest trading port. Traders of tea, coffee, gems from middle east, and spices and leaves from India, opium and porcelain from China, and varieties of metals and new inventions from Europe, Malacca grew leaps and bound to a centre of regional and world trade.

Generation after generation, Malacca slowly began to lose its grip on honesty, safety, education, technology, efficiency. Crime and piracy became rampant. The Sultan and its government were no longer honest. Control over its port was poorly managed. Education and religion treated were no longer priority.

Dhol recalled his uncle once said, a sign of downfall of a great civilization started with a bad leader. If the leader was not able to solve its internal issues, the people will suffer. Greed and arrogance will override humane and nobility values. "History has shown over and over again how grand Muslim empires collapsed and destroyed. Not a single one was caused by Muslim enemies but from internal power abuse and corruption. "When corruption and power abuse is widespread, the strength of the empire weakens and they were eventually brought down and conquered by the enemy," he said

All that is history now. The Portuguese destroyed every single remains of the Islamic civilization had built. Buildings, mosques, administration, and even the palaces burned and flattened. Not even the mortuaries of the warriors like Hang Tuah and his 4 friends are sparred. They tortured, raped and murdered our children. Many villagers fled to neighbouring nations.

The candles lit surrounding the room were reaching its bottom and slowly deeming. Dhol lowered down his voice as master Sam was now fast asleep. Another day is sparred for the prisoners. Dhol left the room feeling sad on thoughts of the realities of Malacca.

Chapter 15 – Kept Well In His Chest .....For Now

Master Sam had made it clear of his intention to travel to Mecca soon. But he was expecting an important person to arrive before his departure. And that would delay the trip by maybe 6, or 7 days. He has no plans of climbing the stairs for the coming days except on the day prior to departure. And that would be to bid goodbye.

In the meantime, he and the troop will not have much to do other than to fill their days to deepen with more knowledge on his faith and roots.

No one knew that master Sam was born and raised as a Muslim. He was taught well. He studied from several famous scholars in Persia and the Jazirah [referred to the soil of Arab Peninsular]. His father was wealthy. During his early twenties, in one of his business trips to northern India, he met a girl, of such beauty that had his head kept rolling for her. They got married. His business grew, and became an empire. He got heavy into alcohol, and shisha, and women, and many more. Around him, obviously enemies were envious of his success. They planned a revenge, with easiest way, alas his consort as the "sacrifice". They made up stories of her infidelity in his absence and spread it maliciously. Being young, wealthy, and powerful, master Sam didn't wait too long to get hooked to the bait. He skinned his wife's face brutally to ensure no one gets her after him. He left her to hang herself several days later. Master Sam was only to be told the truth by his closest advisor, Karl, whom had just arrived from a different location some weeks later. Master Sam fled Nepal with his guards, in search of forgiveness. He regretted, but nothing can reverse what he had done. He wanted to seek repentance. Hence, Adam's Peak.

But let his stories remained in his chest. Until he closed his eyes. And that will take him a long time to do so, even if that were ever to happen.

And he has another discovery! And that he wishes the old wise man may have an answer to it...... It is a completely different subject matter. Master Sam observed Dhol from far through his mask to that...............

Chapter 16 – Dhol's Scribble

It had been 11 days since master Sam had not visited Adam's Peak. Eleven days of waiting for the old wise man, who was said to be arriving to visit master Sam. Dhol and comrades had spent every night worth compiling narrations of great knowledge among themselves.

Dhol felt that it would not be complete should the final and greatest prophet Muhammad narration was not included in their material. But Dhol knew that of the many prophets, Muhammad is the nearest to our generations. His events were the most accurately recorded in the most detailed possible. Prophet Muhammad is the only human in this world that Dhol believe had his life scrutinised and observed every second by his companions and followers. From his thoughts, principles, policies, strategies, businesses, right to his personal life were narrated and adopted. This was the "sunnah" or rather ways of the Rasulullah, in a simple lay man term.

Dhol spent the early morning till the sun was right on top of his head, writing. He had taken some papers back the night before. He had planned to jot some lines prior to any story telling sessions in the coming days. They were told that the old wise man would be arriving today and that master Sam will prioritise his time with the man. Hence no story-telling night for today.

He figured that one moment of time but from a different perspective of the final messenger would help to give a view on struggles and difficulties of Muhammad towards raising the flags of Islam to the world.

Dhol began to scribble……

Let's take back in time during the days of the Prophet Muhammad SAW. There was the Treaty of Hudaibiyah. By the end of the treaty, where the Muslims and Quraish eventually sign the treaty, everybody in the Muslim camp was very upset. A close companion, Omar was so upset that he even raised his voiced at the prophet. Abu Bakar, a man whom had never disputed the prophet since the beginning of his shahadah, too was very upset, that even though Omar raised his voice at Muhammad SAW, Abu Bakar didn't silence him. He let him go. Like it was justified. The rest of the companions, for the first time, collectively disobeyed him. These are simple snippets of how angry, upset, disappointed the Muslims were. Even the prophet himself was deeply upset. Imagine they came all the way from Madinah to perform the Haj, and they weren't allowed to do so. And now they have to return all the way to Madinah without having to perform the rituals. On top of that, to add insult to injury, the animals they brought with them for the sacrifice, were not allowed to be brought back, but to be slaughtered and the meat to be served for the poor, charity and other communities in Mecca. And where does the meat go? None other than the very community that prevented them from performing their Haj rituals. It goes to the Quraish. Not to mention that some of the Muslims who stayed and continued to be tortured by the Quraish in Mecca. In this state, where everybody was upset, at that moment, a new revelation in Suratul Fath was sent to our prophet. The surah described that victory is near, and that changed the whole perception of the umat and sahabat.

Allah sees things that human cannot afford to do so holistically. So, Allah provide Quran for us as guidance and reference. We read Quran, then follow prophet's way of executing it. The study of the Sirah Muhammad is to provide how

Quran is used to shed lights of world events. And that light continues to be shed even until today.

Let's break up the Sirah into simple parts. Up until the age of 40, Rasullullah Muhammad is not a messenger. He is a regular citizen of the Quraish Meccan community. He is known as the most honest, trustworthy person in the community. He has gone through a few major trials of his life. Never met his dad whom passed away even before he was born. The mom died when he was 6. raised as an orphan and transferred in guardianship from the grand dad and later on, his uncle. Later on in life, he gets good in business and got married and have children.

The next chapter of his life was when he became prophet. He started preaching the people. And in this period, the first part of it, was when he was made fun of, he is not believed. But there were still no violent actions taken against him. People dismissed of what he was saying. They think he has gone crazy, lost his mind, some even feel sorry for him. But it was not like he has enemies at this point of time.

The chapter after was when people started to believe in what he said. They began to realize that he was not crazy, some believed him, he won't give up, and there are more and more people starting to believe in what he preaches on. And some of the very valued young people, whom the Quraish thought would have great careers ahead of them, are beginning to align with him.   The Quraish sees it as becoming a problem. Now they have to warn the community to not listen to him. Simply because he is forming a cult. So, there was actually a more active campaign against him, to under-mind his character, dismiss what he was doing, to dissuade other people from listening to him. If he walks to the marketplace to start preaching the words of Quran, many attempts done to make a lot of noise, distract people, so that they don't get influenced by Muhammad. The early tactics for people to get away from Quran is by playing loud music. They would actually hire female singers, good dancers, throw some open concert and money to distract. It worked then and still works today.

From there leads us to the 3rd chapter. He is not distracted. The Quraish character assassination didn't work, they were not successful to convince people to not listen to him. None of the propaganda worked. More and more believed him, the followers grew. The Quraish had to solve this problem by other means. It got physical. And when things became physical, the companions who didn't have immigration rights are among those that got the first wrath, especially those non-Arabs who didn't have Arab citizenships. Hence among the first oppressors are the immigrants. And then they go after the poor. And the they try to intimidate the young. That's what they did then and they still do it today, with tortures, beatings, discriminations, threats. It reached to a point where they were ready to kill the prophet SAW himself. Despite the power, media, military, propaganda, money were under their control, Islam kept on spreading. Therefore, the only way to stop the spread of Islam then is by killing the prophet. The plot to assassinate him did not materialise as Allah sent his messenger to leave town.

In Madinah, Muhammad had a bunch of supporters. This led to the next chapter. Given the agenda, Muhammad's main task is to cleanse the house of Allah in Mecca. Muhammad was fully aware whether he likes it or not, he needs to protect his people from harassment, being killed, total annihilation. Cold war and embargos were taking place. Having these happenings, large and more outside world were beginning to realise how legitimate the threats of Muslims to the Quraish. So many tribes from other parts of Arabia began to join Muhammad. They want to hear about Islam, curious about Islam. There was no greater change in the world history other than the one brought by the Messenger of Allah, Muhammad. It was the greatest revolution, transformation ever. They were mentally, spiritually, economically, politically, socially different from the Meccan within a span of 23 years. This was unprecedented. And all happened and executed by none other than our prophet, Muhammad SAW.

In short summary, We are here, live, breath, able to talk, preach, benefited, as Muslims, all as a product of the hard work revolutionized by Muhammad SAW and his companions.

Dhol suddenly remembered that Master Sam is expecting a visitor today. "I need to stop writing for now. This can continue later."

Chapter 17 – Old Wise Man's Story

Dhol approached the sacred footprint area to have a glimpse of who the old man that he was told to be meeting master Sam. Dhol heard from some locals that the old man was a successful businessman, through which he uses his wealth to acquire knowledge from famous historians with great book collections. He was also a very prominent religious scholar from Persia. He happened to be in this area. And was invited to share his knowledge in private. Dhol walked closer to the shaded area and carried with him a sack of gunny pretending to pick up some stuff. He approached the nearest spot close enough to hear their conversation. Some bushes thick enough to hide him from the two gentlemen's visibility.

Master Sam greeted the old man in white robe and headgear by bowing slightly. Master Sam with thick eye bags did not wait long to begin his curiosity. "Tell me more of this," asked master Sam while pointing to the footprint with his right thumb [In the east culture, it was a respectable manner for the young to address or ask the elder about a specific object or direction by pointing it using his right thumb].

The old man, having thick white beard, seemed calm, smiled, full of confidence, wisdom glowed from his eyes. He invited master Sam for a sitting along his side with both legs crisscrossing yoga styled. He seemed to have been briefed of master Sam's plight and agony. He didn't wait too long before starting his story.

"This footprint is nothing more than just a symbol. But the understanding of the beginning of humankind is more essential for the next generations to survive with clear conscience and knowledge." the old man began.

"My intention is to introduce our forefather, Adam. And why it is important for us to know and understand the story of Adam, being the earliest lesson in history of the humankind. And I want to share with you 2 stories. It may sound that these stories have nothing to do with each other and a bit silly initially, but at the end of it, we will understand the significance of why things happened.

Imagine for a moment when you woke up today without any re-collection of your life except for whatever that has happened in the last 24 hours. You don't know who your parents are, your name, your history, your hometown, and a lot of other stuff. Frankly, to us, if you do not know your name and family and basic information, you practically do not know yourself. Your sense of identity is very much tied to your sense of the past. That is a simple fact. Hence not having a record of your past is loss of your sense of identity.

 The Al Mighty Creator provides human with proper guidance, along with a book. In many parts of The Book, The Al Mighty emphasizes the importance of history. And in many parts of the history, The Al Mighty describes all human and the whole earth was originally derived from one nation. The entire human living on this earth is like one body. It is like one gigantic group of population living under a single nation. Not knowing its history means not knowing our roots. Likewise, anyone who is a member of our nation but do not know our past actually don't know who we are.

 My other motivation of telling this story is to benefit many of us who did not have the opportunity or raised without formal education on history of mankind, particularly passed down from one generation to another without proper basis of reference. Hence the facts got distorted and twisted and misunderstood. Thus, resulting to a different interpretation and acceptance. As years go by, the history ended completely different from the original version. Which obviously causes humans to vary in opinion. To correct these facts, a new book via revelation of 23 years was sent down for all of mankind to use as guidance. Else, changes made whether ignorantly or on purpose in the past can be corrected and perfected. Similarly, if you have false information about your past, your sense of identity becomes false.

In The Holy Book Al Quran, The Al Mighty said, " We settled you down in the land, and we placed you on this earth with lots of means of life to live well." "This, in other words means, not just to live, but furnished for human to live really well with luxury, comfort and health."

But now comes the question. Why did Al Mighty the Creator put human on this earth? A simple and fundamental answer is.... For us to be thankful, grateful, appreciative of this life.

Now, we switch to the 2nd story. Let's take a different situational perspective. Imagine a young man who got his first job. An entry level position doing very basic works that lower ranked employees usually do. He is just grateful to have the job and willing to do whatever the owner instructs him to do so. And then later on he gets promoted to one level higher. And then another level and so on. As years go by, as he continues to dedicate years of his life with the same company, he keeps getting promoted for the good job he did and recognized as the best employee throughout the years. Until he became the highest ranked officer in the organization, just one spot below the owner of the company.

Then one day, the boss introduced a teenage kid to this guy and said," I'd like you to meet our new member. He is taking your job, and that you are to report to him from now onwards."

If you were viewing this scenario, you can imagine what is going to happen. The poor guy earned his spot with all the hard work and sacrifice. And the kid, what does he know about work? This is not fair, unjust! Any sane and normal person would sympathize with the guy. How could the boss do this to the most loyal and faithful employee?

Let's put this in the context of man versus angels. Can man be at par with angels when it comes to loyalty and obedience to God? Angels were created from fire, being subservient without any hesitation and question. On the other hand, human was created from soil, mud, clay and dust. Man, can either choose to be less or, even more obedient to God that surpasses angels.

Allah created this magnificent creation called man and wanted all angels to bow as in respect to Adam. Not to bow to Adam, but bow because man is such an amazing creation that angels should be humbled how creative Allah to have had created Adam. At this juncture, all angels bow with humility except for Iblis. Iblis couldn't accept that Adam who was created from soil should gain respect from angels.

Reflecting to the story about the guy who got promoted for all the hard work done over many years of service, and mapping it with Iblis the Devil, something needs a deeper look at this issue. What is it that Iblis would get if the position was not given to Adam? Would Iblis get wealth, good life, or was he trying to please Allah? Or could it be that Iblis wanted recognition and appreciation?

It is natural that human gets a pat on the back for a job well done. Even our prophets recognized and appreciated his comrades for their commitment and dedication. But Al

Mighty knows its creations. The Creator knows what its creations show and hide inside. Iblis in particular, has not been sincere. Iblis did not do all the tasks for Al Mighty, instead for recognition.

If you do things for the right reason, and gets appreciated, that is fine. But if you do them to get recognition, it is completely a different thing. The desire to get recognized, appreciated, may lead to arrogance. If you do things for appreciation, it is a completely different thing.

There are several common things between Adam and Iblis.
1. They were both unique creations, given special ranks. Supreme rank for Iblis amongst the angel, while Adam as Caliph or leader of the earth.
2. Later, they both disobeyed Allah.

But what is the difference between the two?

Adam admitted his mistakes and repented in humility. Iblis, refused to admit. Instead, he sought for revenge.

When Iblis refused to bow [perform sajdah] as a sign of respect for Allah's greatest creation, as in human, it signalled the rest of the angels that

Iblis felt he is better than Adam. His status is higher. He was made from fire. The point that Iblis forgot that all in this universe are Allah's creation, it is only Allah that can decide who is better than the other. It is not us who has the right to classify of such.

Very similarly, Iblis wants us to forget who created us. Iblis wanted us to compare who is better than the other. Iblis wants us to be like him. The entire obsession of comparing oneself to another creation. Doing so will make us continuously go against each other. When Iblis said he is made from fire while Adam from clay, Iblis has succeeded to instil deep comparison among human of the type of clay that each of us were created from. White clay, yellow, brown, black etc. About skin colour, race, countries, region, working class, wealth, looks, and many more. This idea of comparisons will constantly start shaping your thoughts and what you do in your life. And what your priorities are. Moving from one generation to another, Iblis has successfully made us obsessed with comparisons. Such obsession is so powerful that obeying Allah has disappeared. Even when Allah confronted Iblis directly asking what prevented Iblis from adhering to Allah's command, Iblis is so consumed to comparing to Adam that Iblis forgot to apologize. Instead, Iblis comparison to

Adam had led him to jealousy. Iblis cannot accept that Adam is smarter and appointed as the Caliph of the earth. Iblis vowed to destroy Adam and all his generations to come and bring along with him to hellfire and doom. That led Iblis to constantly feel upset that he is not chosen. As a result, he kept finding ways to pull Adam down, diverting his focus to do evil from good. Knowing so well that he is heading to hellfire, Adam cannot go to heaven. It is about the disease in your heart. Iblis is consumed by rage.

 To shorten the story, Iblis is commanded to be expelled from heaven. Iblis has lost his ranked, he is about to be pushed out from the closeness of Allah. At that point, he responds to Allah. And this was how Iblis eventually got the nickname "Syaitan". It is important to understand the meaning and how the word "Syaitan" came into being. From Arabic language, one of the meaning is "Someone who goes far far away". Another meaning, also in Arabic refers to "Someone who is engulfed in flames because of anger, or his heart is on fire, ablazed associated with temper and has gone too far in his hate". So, Iblis, as he is being sentenced for expulsion, had appealed to Allah to allow him to do one thing, and that he is allowed to do it till the end of time. Iblis said, "Give me extra time until the day of resurrection, to whisper to human to disobey Allah." It is this opportunity that Iblis used to proof to Allah that he is not the only failure. He successfully persuaded Adam and many of Adam's children and generations to conduct all that are against Allah's commands. And that includes us. He knows for a fact that he cannot avoid punishment. And he blamed Allah for what happened. Worse still, he doesn't want to be alone. Iblis and his minions will wait for Adam and his children and ambush them to go astray. And that was exactly what happened to Adam. Iblis openly announced to Allah that his strategy to deviate human is by attacking them from front, back, left and right. That practically from all angles, so to speak.

Having said that, Iblis forgot that Allah, being The Creator, is always uncountable steps ahead. Human makes mistakes. But so long as you repent and seek forgiveness, there is a way to be back on the right track. And where do you seek for forgiveness? "ABOVE" in which Iblis cannot attack you. For as long as you are still breathing the air, your eyes wide open, listening to the chirp of birds, able to cry, and your heart still beating....you still have the chance to seek for forgiveness. And that was exactly what Adam did. And many more after him. "

The old wise man paused for a while. He then continued while looking sharp to master Sam, "You are no different. You were raised and taught to lead the family, community, organization. Your actions will have its impact to all within your circle. What you sow is what you reap. Virtue gives you happiness. Vice versa, it gives you pain. You and only you knew what you have done. You can lie to others but not to yourself. Look in the mirror. Reflect the years that you have gone through. Who and what and where and why and how. And then....

And with that, I will leave you for today to ponder of how much love Allah has given you despite all our shortcomings as a weak, arrogant and ungrateful creature.

The old man left while master Sam in un-consolable tears reflecting his past.

Chapter 18 - The Dream

Master Sam could not stop crying even long after the old man left. Dhol could not control himself too, having feeling emotional from seeing master Sam that he started crying quietly from the bushes where he was hiding. Dhol didn't realize that his friends were also witnessing the whole episode from within reach. Sombre mood surrounded the hill that day that no one noticed time passed by till the next dawn.

....
....

The clouds were widely hovering at Adam's Peak. It was almost zero visibility. Cold dark dawn. Dhol was awakened by a touch on his shoulder. It was master Sam. 'Why are you sleeping here?" asked master Sam. "And you must have a bad dream. Your cry, I could hear it from the shades." he said further while pointing to the Adam's footprint shade. To that, Dhol woke up and hugged master Sam. "I had a very sad dream. I saw an old man in white. He was talking to you. It was right there under the shade." "Tell me, I want to hear every single bit," said master Sam anxiously.

Dhol wept his tears, still sobbing intermittently. He walked slowly in the dark following master Sam closer towards the shade. Master Sam had put on his mask again as he turned to walk away from the dark. That was a missed opportunity for Dhol to be able to see his real face. But he couldn't. That was a miss.

They sat on the floor leaning to the wall at the east pillar structure. With some light from the tiny candle placed near the footprint, master Sam waited for Dhol to share his dream. Dhol re-tied his long white turban like cloth around his head. He began. " I saw an old man talking to you. His face resembles me, except he was some 30 years older than me. My mind kept saying that that was me seeing myself in years to come. It was a conversation the old man had with you, master. But a lesson that we all can learn from too." " I can clearly remember word by word of the old man's message to you. Here was how it goes."

"It was a cold and quiet night. The clouds were thick, hovering around this mountain top. It wasn't so clear as the light from the torch was nearing its end. No one else around. It was here at this very shade. I saw an old man approached you. He was as tall as us both, a bit slouch, white beard, well dressed, had a tasbih in his palm. He had his hand touching your shoulder blade. The old man said," My days in this world are numbered. I must let you know that there is another one of you with the exact same birthmark at his shoulder blade. He was your elder brother. Find him," and the old man just vanished.

 "And I was just here too, not knowing where I came from. But I was here. I can't walk, talk, move, waive, breath. Just witnessed, but helpless."

The two gentlemen were speechless thereafter. No words can describe their minds. Complete silence. Only the wind breezed and clouds waived.

 A little later, they heard footsteps heading closer to them.............

Chapter 19 - Finding Peace In Pain

Old man stepped into the shades, holding a brownish scripture, the size slightly larger than his palm. The book looks like it's been over-used and almost torn all over. Dhol and master Sam were still in deep child cries that does not look like it will end that soon. From his facial expression, the old man sensed that master Sam was at the edge of a cliff. His cries described of his full sense of remorse.

This is the 3rd and final day of the old man visiting master Sam, with the intention of bidding farewell. Old man has a mission, to meet and spread the words of Salaam to the world, whom ever has an open heart to listen to him.

"Ehmmm grmm,' the old man as if adjusting his throat sounded like. Signalling to the men of his presence but didn't look comforting from far for now. He came closer and kneeled by, next to the gentlemen. "My child", patting on master Sam's shoulder gently.

"Allah teaches in His book, that there is one thing that if you can get it in your life, it is more valuable than everything else. Everything will be fine if you get this one thing. And that one thing is closeness to Allah." He continued," And be good to Allah". "And truly developing a connection and a bond with Him. The problem with people is they get distracted when life is good, and only good. We fill our minds with money, power, women, allocates priority for creating empire of wealth and status. They are all good, and nothing is wrong to do so, only if they are for good causes. Our Creator, unfortunately then, is not in the picture. There's no Allah left.   It is you chilling. That is all there is.

"And then times get tough. And the friends are not there. And the laughter and drinks doesn't feel and taste good anymore. Something tragic happened. For some, the health is gone. When the health is gone, none of those things mean anything anymore. For some, their loved ones were taken. And all due to our own hands. All the things that you lived for. Because of this one blessing that Allah diminished for you a little bit. At that point, you have 2 options. If you are these people that are on the cliff, on the edge, you may start complaining to Allah," Why did you do this to me? You didn't like that I was happy?".

 "Or you can earn the greatest treasure you and I can earn"." And that is humility and closeness to Allah."

 Dhol and master Sam were dead silence listening. Eyes red, teary, staring to the ground, in deep thoughts. Kamil, Noah and Ilham whom earlier sneaked closer to the shades, had hid behind stacks of planks nearby too, listening, attentively. All had their eyes soaked in tears, feeling stabbed straight to the hearts.

 Old man continued," To actually realize when we were healthy, when we had all the power, women, wealth, health, status, we didn't realize that even then we were on life support. Allah was providing us everything in every moment. We didn't earn anything on our own. None of it were something that we deserved. This is why Allah said, "Those will have a share of what they have earned." you can't really earn something. It is a favour from Allah whatever he has given you. But we didn't realize it at that time, it just come easy. But then you start begging Allah, and asking Allah and crying to Allah. And praying to Allah like you have never prayed before. Feeling closer to Him like you have never felt before. And then Allah heals you. And then you realized those moments you had, when no one supported you, you're all alone crying for help, were the sweetest moments of your entire life. Those were a few of moments that you actually had nothing between you and your Creator. And those might be the moments that saved you in the hereafter. That might be the biggest gift that Allah has ever given you."

"But for some people who are on the edge, when times get tough, they turn their faces away. What does that mean? It means they want nothing to do with their Creator. How can He abandon me? How can He give me a hard time? Why would He do that to me?"

" This is actually very easy to understand. For those with power and wealth, everything becomes effortless, instantaneous, quick, easy. But now you make do'a and ask from Allah. You expect Allah to take care of some of your problems. But when it doesn't happen that quick, you blame your Creator. You turn your face, blaming Him for he didn't solve your problem. "

"We need to understand that Allah has a plan for everybody. And just to give a comparison, in the case of Prophet Jacob [Yaakub] who lost his child [Yusuf]. Allah returned his child to him after many years. And in the case of Musa, his mother also lost her child. But was returned to her after a few hours. Because by the time the child got hungry, the next feeding was from the same mother. What am I trying to get at? Sometimes in this world, Allah will relieve that pain of yours immediately. Sometimes he will relieve it after many years. But in all of it there's good. In the case of Yusuf, all those years his father cried, while Yusuf became a child servant and then got jailed for wrongful accusations. And in that jail was when Yusuf was asked to interpret the king's dream of the entire economy collapsing in 7 years. Yusuf was the only one who has sound knowledge and knows how to handle that crisis. He was appointed the Chief Treasurer of the nation. He eventually got reunited with his dad and whole family. Had he not been in jail, he would have never helped the king. Had he not been away from the family, he wouldn't have help to save thousands of citizens, children from starvation. One father cried for several years, but his tears, Allah made them a way of saving thousands of families from crying. Because if he didn't save the economy, the entire land would have been in drought." " Sometimes the difficulty you go through isn't just better for you, maybe through your difficulties, you will become an ongoing charity for so many others.

....
....

"This is what I want to leave you with," old man pulled master Sam up to stand, hugged him, and hand him over the palm size scripture. It was a long hug that master Sam did not want to let go. He began to wet the old man's shoulder with his tears.

....
....

Dhol got up. His friends stood by some distance. None of them was of any interest to allow the old man to depart. Not this soon. So much had they gain. But it is just not enough. Not the time yet for the old man to just disappear, leaving them with knowledge half cook. But, as much as they wanted, old man's journey is endless. Dhol and all had to accept it. They bid farewell in the most and best of relationship. Ever.

Chapter20 - Connection, almost.......

"Krrrpppp", tree branches being stepped onto. Dhol is not perturbed by the distractions around him. Both his hands were still neatly raised upwards in prayers while tears flow freely. It was Old wise man. He had every moment of intent to speak to Dhol but couldn't find suitable to. But now he had no time left before his carriage leaves to the next destination.

Old man waited till Dhol was over and done with his do'a. "My dear son, I didn't travel this far aimlessly. As a matter of fact, I have been tracking you with a message that I have kept too long," he exclaimed. Dhol slowly wept his face but didn't turn immediately to look at the old wise man. He waited to hear more, while still kneeling on his sejadah. Old wise man continued, "I met....."

Old wise man suddenly woke up from his dream. He had waited long for this. But too nervous when the opportunity knocks.

Chapter 21 - The Journey Through India

They were finally set for the journey.

As their carriages rolled onto the southernmost soil of India at Danushkodi Port, they passed through a busy and noisy street market filled with snakes charming, spices and cloves, colorful sarees and turbans, and young mothers with newly born children in their arms begging for food and drinks. The caravans had to move very slowly while the guards shoo away pedestrians and petty traders from blocking their passage.

Dhol has, in the past, seen some Indian merchants who travelled to Malacca to perform Snake Charming, a practice of appearing to hypnotize a snake by playing and waving around an instrument called a pungi. A typical performance also includes handling the snakes or performing other seemingly dangerous acts, as well as other street performance staples, like juggling and sleight of hand.

As they passed the port city towards a narrow path, Karl instructed the troop to slow down as to seek direction from the locals for the city of Goa. Dhol peeped from his cell carriage. A loud voice speaking in Tamil was heard explaining. Head nodding, hand movements, with full expression.... Truly Indian signature.

Ilham and mates came closer to Dhol to view the outside scenery. "Goa will be some 3 weeks ride from here, according to the locals. We have time to prepare more stories for master Sam, hopefully," said Ilham, as he translates the conversation had between the local and Karl, the voices heard from far away.

....
....

Afar from the carriage, some locals were having spitting challenge. It was a common thing to observe individuals across the land, who would spit out their saliva after enjoying a munch of betel leaves folded with areca nuts, tobacco and white powder. Dhol smiled as he spotted two local men competing in a betel leaf chewing and spitting challenge. A unique game indeed.
Somehow, at far end of the road, the 4 friends saw a group of well-dressed men walking towards the caravan in a rush manner. The

elderly men in the middle of the group looks as if he is the leader, walking surrounded and protected by the younger and bigger size rookies. As colorful as the longies they wore, the swords they carry seemed prominent in size and weight. Footsteps sounded as if they were marching drew closer. The men stopped and spoke to Karl. Some minutes later, one of the guards seen coming towards Dhol and friends. "Ilham, you are out."

Dhol and friends looked at each other. Ilham turned back after an hour to bid farewell. Those men were sent by his family. They had come to bring him home. He, apparently is the youngest of a wealthy plantation owner. His family managed to track Ilham much earlier, even at the Adam's Peak. But it was Ilham who had requested to stay back with the friends as he realized of the knowledge he gained from his days in captivity.

"I've got good news," smiled Ilham while grinning to Dhol and the others. "My dad has agreed to allow you and the whole master Sam's caravan to use a vessel of ours for your journey to Mecca, for free. I will not travel with you. But I managed to convince my family for you to use the vessel, having so much that I've learned from the 3 months I spent with you. So, you will get down from here and jump into "Noah", our family vessel. It should fit for all. My only request is that you must return to meet me on your way home. I want to hear about your journey. I want to hear it all."

The friends again had a tearful farewell. This was never in the plan. Things are turning good every step of the way. Dhol can only raise his hands up praying in gratitude for all the gifts he and the rest had received from The Al Mighty. SubhanAllah.

Chapter 22 -
"Gratitude", an advise from Luqman The Wise

It didn't take long after the caravan had turn to the port of Danushkodi that they bumped into the old wise man on his horse. Along with the wise man was another horse, but without a rider. Just some carriage that he brought along on it. Probably for his supplies or so. "He must have left a little later from the Serendib Island for other matters, it seemed," thought Dhol. Dhol and friends observed him passing their carriage cell heading towards master Sam's.

Wise man had Karl taken him into master Sam's caravan. They spent a while. Dhol recalled of his tiny book, wondering its whereabout. Must have lost it somewhere. He will have to start with a new book then.

Karl later came and asked Dhol to come out of the cell, leaving Kamil and Noah wondering if they will be left to continue the journey without 2 of their newly found best of friends. It turned

out that their guess was spot on. Master Sam
had agreed to have Dhol to accompany the wise
man via inland route to Mecca. It seemed that it
was the way of master Sam saying thank you to
the old wise man. By now, Dhol got to know
that the old wise man's name was Luqman. And
they will take the route passing through
northwest of India and stopping over in Persia.
They will then cross straits of Hormuz and reach
the southeast of the Arabian Peninsular before
heading to Mecca.

Dhol had no choice other than to follow as he
was without money and knowledge of his
whereabouts. It was only his will to find his dad
that had brought him there till now.

Dhol and friends bid farewell for they wouldn't
know if they will ever meet again. Even Karl
couldn't bear the touching moments that he
turned his face away to not be seen of his
sadness.

Now that Dhol was about to leave, he rode
along the other horse that Luqman had brought
along, passing though master Sam's caravan.
Dhol saw a man in there that looked like him,
may not be that clear as it was from his side

ways. He turned back but he can no longer see the man. Perhaps it was just in his mind. Dhol left without saying goodbye to master Sam. He wanted to, but Luqman said they were in a rush to reach the nearest town before the sun set. Else it'll be very dark to travel.

That night, Dhol and Luqman arrived at a very small town with just a row of buildings. They were lucky to find a shop that was about to close, that they bought some fruits and canai bread.

Under the dim fire that Luqman lit, he began to open up his personal and private life.

"I have a child, less I have not met him for the last 10 years. I had not performed my rightful duties as a father that my son had gone wrong in his life. I have just found him back recently and I am so blessed to Allah to have taken care of him and brought him back to the righteous path.

As I read suratul Luqman 31: verses 17 and 18, I will adopt to the utmost of my life to correct what I did not do in the past with tender and care."

يَـٰبُنَىَّ أَقِمِ ٱلصَّلَوٰةَ وَأْمُرْ بِٱلْمَعْرُوفِ وَٱنْهَ عَنِ ٱلْمُنكَرِ وَٱصْبِرْ عَلَىٰ مَآ أَصَابَكَ إِنَّ ذَٰلِكَ مِنْ عَزْمِ ٱلْأُمُورِ ﴿١٧﴾

"O my son, establish prayer, enjoin what is right, forbid what is wrong, and be patient over what befalls you. Indeed, [all] that is of the matters [requiring] determination."

وَلَا تُصَعِّرْ خَدَّكَ لِلنَّاسِ وَلَا تَمْشِ فِي ٱلْأَرْضِ مَرَحًا إِنَّ ٱللَّهَ لَا يُحِبُّ كُلَّ مُخْتَالٍ فَخُورٍ ﴿١٨﴾

"And do not turn your cheek [in contempt] towards people and do not walk through the earth exultantly. Indeed, Allah does not like those self-deluded and boastful."

I have learned a great deal from this surah, which happened to have the same name as I am. Indeed, I felt as if this particular surah was directed to me. I felt called to recite and go deeper in my understanding specifically on ayat 31:12 which read:

وَلَقَدْ ءَاتَيْنَا لُقْمَـٰنَ ٱلْحِكْمَةَ أَنِ ٱشْكُرْ لِلَّهِ وَمَن يَشْكُرْ فَإِنَّمَا يَشْكُرُ لِنَفْسِهِ وَمَن كَفَرَ فَإِنَّ ٱللَّهَ غَنِىٌّ حَمِيدٌ ﴿١٢﴾

"And We had certainly given Luqman wisdom [and said], "Be grateful to Allah." And whoever is grateful for [the benefit of] himself. And whoever denies [His favour] – then indeed, Allah is Free of need and Praiseworthy."

I summarized the following as the key points from it:

- There is a time and place to speak to everyone. Luqman spoke to his son when the right time comes
- Part of being a wise person is that any situation you've ever been given is that you find something to be grateful for in every situation that you've have been put into
- Belief in Allah doesn't just mean belief in the entity, the being that is Allah. It leads to certain kinds of attitudes. The first of these attitudes is gratitude, positivity and appreciation that lead to your mentality shifting.

"And whoever is grateful/thankful then certainly he is grateful/thankful for himself. And whoever is ungrateful then certainly Allah is completely Independent, Praiseworthy."

Allah doesn't need people to praise Him! If there was no creation, if nothing had ever been made to praise Him, He would still be worthy of praise, it's part of His quality of creator.

You don't thank Him for every breath you breathe,
You don't thank Him for every vessel in your body that's being filled with blood that flows through your veins
You don't thank Him for every heart-beat, but He still allows it
The fact that you and I can see, and blink, and hear... all of that are from Allah and he never asked for you to praise Him. But you praise Him as an expression of gratitude to thank Him for the gifts

Dhol listened attentively despite wanting to know more about Luqman and what actually happened to his son. But he allowed time to let it flow by itself.

Chapter 23 - Noah, the Vessel

Meanwhile, master Sam and his travelling caravan finally completed their on-loading of carriage unto the vessel at Port Danushkodi. He thanked Ilham and the family for their generosity to spare the transport along with the crew and captain. He apologized and seek forgiveness from Ilham and the family as well for having kept Ilham with bad treatment for months. Ilham seemed calm. Ilham knew that the dad was well informed of the whole situation, even without the knowledge of master Sam. Master Sam thanked the family again for he can never repay their kindness. Ilham assured him earlier that it was for free in exchange for their return visit and a copy of the book with stories compilation upon its completion. Ilham was very thankful to master Sam for kidnapping him and keeping him for that 3 months period for he would have continued to be a spoiled kid, wasting his parents' wealth aimlessly and without purpose in life. He now has clear conscience and will dedicate his life to study the history of civilization of mankind. He promised to learn several other languages including Malay, Arabic and Persian. They then bid farewell. The crew joined him to wave goodbye from the rear end of the ship as it sailed towards south Indian Ocean.

Master Sam now has 2 "Noahs" close to him. One, a former prisoner of his that turned an important contributor to the book in progress being compiled. Another, is the vessel borrowed from Ilham's family named "Little Noah". Master Sam walked around to view every section of the vessel, acknowledging the beauty of the ship, its size, design, stability, and appearance. Sometime ago, he heard someone mentioned how the Noah's Ark was constructed many generations earlier. He went down to the lower deck level and saw tens of compartments with wire mash nets. Most likely, these are nets used as doors cum windows for the plants that Ilham's family use to transport their crops and plants from one location to another. Perhaps the name was given to reflect the concept of Noah's Ark where compartments were meant to house the several thousand animals of each species during the great flood.

Master Sam found a section of the vessel at the upper floor that looked like a study room, having book shelves, writing material and papers, chairs and tables. Sufficient for a size of

6 people. The room had a window with good and bright view of the ocean. He decided to start writing a new chapter of the book, "Noah".

....

....

Master Sam remembered well of his Ustaz's teachings. In Arabic language, Nuh means "The one who remain". In Hebrew, it refers to a person who stays, who sits. Pretty close in meaning between the two. From scholars' perspective, Nuh or Noah remained among his people whilst continuously reminding them of the righteous path. He didn't give up nor did he lose hope. According to historians, Noah lived for 950 years or so.

Noah's story occurred probably more than 6 thousand years ago. Noah lived some 10 generations after Adam. Whether there was civilization other than the one in his nation, it was not clearly known. The fact remains that after tens of years of preaching, his people is only interested to listen, but not adhere [Nuh 71:7].

وَإِنِّي كُلَّمَا دَعَوْتُهُمْ لِتَغْفِرَ لَهُمْ جَعَلُوا أَصَابِعَهُمْ فِي آذَانِهِمْ وَاسْتَغْشَوْا ثِيَابَهُمْ وَأَصَرُّوا وَاسْتَكْبَرُوا اسْتِكْبَارًا ۝

"And indeed, every time I invited them that You may forgive them, they put their fingers in their ears, covered themselves with their garments, persisted, and were arrogant with [great] arrogance."

And as he looked at the rough sea, master Sam remembered another great prophet named Yunus, but that will be a chapter of his own, perhaps later.

The 1st night on the vessel arrived. The men were called to the library for master Sam had wanted to continue sharing more of his lessons taught by his former teacher, Ustaz Nouman on prophet Nuh's struggles that he recited from surah Nuh. In Dhols' absence, Noah was appointed as chief of scripting.

Kamil and Noah had a shock of their lives as they entered the room. Indeed, they saw the real face of master Sam. Master Sam had removed his mask. They were stunned, startled, confused, surprised, speechless. Is this for real? Or are you ....

Chapter 24 - The Route Map

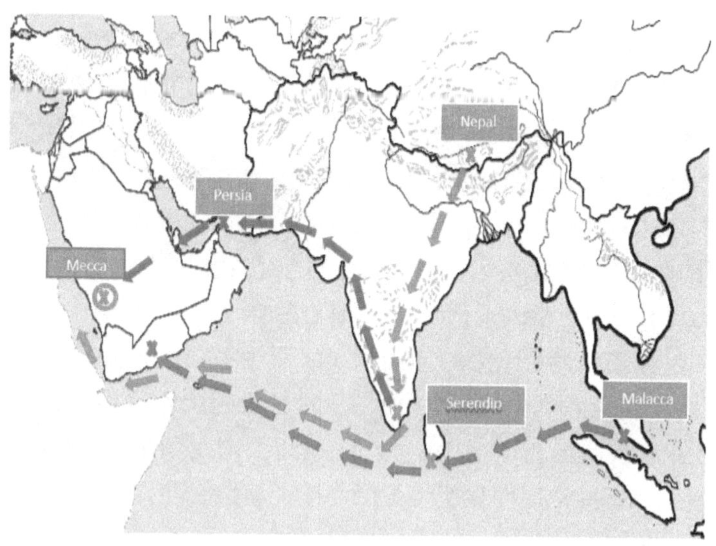

A sketch of part of Asia map showing route from Malacca to Mecca. Dhol's original planned sea route in thick red line. Master Sam started his journey from Nepal, embossed in green thick line. Dhol eventually followed "Luqman The Wise" and had taken the blue line as the actual inland route instead. Mecca is circled in green.

Chapter 25 - Not Aladdin, it's Al-Addeen

A bearded vulture circles around the edge of straits of Hormuz, within distance from where Dhol and Luqman are riding. Soon enough, they came across a middle age man who stood by his camel. "He's dying," shouted the man while wiping his tears in Persian language. The old dromedary camel looks helpless lying on its left side with its knees bleeding. The man waived as a signal asking for help. "Got bitten by a rattle snake some miles back,' he added pointing to the camel's left leg. Luqman wait no longer. He waived to the man, then tapped on his horse's back, as if hinting the man to jump on it and waste no more time. The sun was not in any compromise moment, and no one would want to die standing in the middle of it.

Dhol and Luqman got down and hastily assisted the man to end his camel's life. They take turn to scoop sand using the leather saddle taken from the camel to bury the poor animal.

It's a challenge to deafen their ears as the vulture didn't stop groaning for food while surrounding the aerial vicinity.

The man grabbed his shaggy leather bag pack and hopped quickly onto Luqman's back. They continued the journey a little longer approaching Bandar Kartan, nearest point to cross from Persia to the Arabian Peninsular.
As they reached Kartan, Dhol smiled at the man and jokingly said," You should have just use Persian flying carpet to travel. It'll swuusshh in no time." The man pretended to ignore Dhol and pointed to a row of shops approaching. "Let's stop there for food. It'll be on me. Thank you for your generosity, gentlemen."
They got down at the shed adjacent to the shop, given some water to wash their face and hands, and adjourned to the shop. "welcome ya Sahibul Syeikh," wish a well-dressed man from the shop as though they knew each other very well. They shook hands and kiss. The shop owner showed the way to a reserved-cubicles within its private corner at far end. "Please bring your best dishes of the day. I have these gentlemen along whom I'm indebted to midway my journey," he said to the shop owner.

"You look like a traveller in search for a long overdue answer," the man looked at Dhol straight to his face. Before Dhol could start talking, the man continued," I always share this explanation to everyone I met so they have the right understanding of the concept of flying carpet. Persian carpets are a symbol of skills, identity, prestige, respect, quality, smoothness. It takes pride to own one. And flying refers to high above all, ability to do way beyond others, uninterrupted, flowing freely, smooth. Persians are great in governance, process, empathy. When the Aladdin was added to the flying and or magic carpet, it gives a much greater and larger concept. It refers to a character with good heart having the ability to travel far in short distance to help others." to this, the man stopped as their food arrived. Shish kebabs, lamb stew, samosas, falafel, sour shrimp, and pickles were served.

"Now, the term Aladdin, should be correctly pronounced as "Al-Addeen", would mean much more accurate and makes more sense. Al-Addeen literally refers to "Way of Life", the way we should adopt in every step of our daily routines, principles, policies, constitution. Al-Addeen is the highest level of virtues of life. It reflects the path that all our forefathers have been preaching their communities, as well as us into. The path was duly encrypted in all the scriptures bestowed onto men since the beginning of life." "Now my young man, when Aladdin and his flying carpet was introduced to this world, it was supposed to be a reflection of how smooth and efficient an Islamic government executes it responsiblilities according to the guidelines and principles of Islam for its citizens regardless of ethnicities, religion, backgrounds, and colours that cares, monitors, empathizes, protects, listens and guides the needs of each and every soul and walks of life on this earth. And all that based on adopting the guidance and principles of the original scriptures, the word of our Creator."

"It is so heart breaking to observe and notice all across the globe that Aladdin and his flying carpet is made fun of, regarded by the young as a children's character of myth, propagated by adults with intent to derail the overall noble concept from its true fundamentals."

"With that, I end. In all my honesty, I am thankful for your help in the desert, without which I may be subject to as the meal of the day for the vultures. Assalamualaikum."

The man left, with the shop patron accompanying him towards the exit. The patron came back ensuring Dhol and Luqman that the bills are covered. And that the man was the regional governor who made his rounds in territories under his supervision regularly. He was a well-respected servant of AlMighty who has diligently ensured the wealth of the nation is distributed to good use for the last two decades.

Dhol, feeling embarrassed and ashamed for his remarks, was clearly seen from his sombre facial expression. " The slip of your tongue fortunately earn you good knowledge and lesson, young man," gasped Luqman while still crunching some pistachios.

"Let's get some rest tonight. I have something very important to show you tomorrow before we depart to the peninsular of Al Arabia."

There they stood in front of a cemetery with a dusty oval shaped stone, probably one to be recognized only by those very close to the dead. No indication that the graveyard has been visited lately. No wind, sun as angry as ever without the slightest cloud shading the soil. It was a flat land of hard rocks and sands. A common cemetery view around the middle eastern region where one bid stone with some scribbles of names is used as indication of the who the deceased were.

"My son, I have a confession to make," Luqman's voice a little soft and sombre. "Some thirty years ago, I fled the land of Malacca during the Portuguese invasion. We headed here, Persia my home town. Along, I brought with me my dearest friend, my business partner, a man of principles who taught me unaccountable knowledge on life, Quran, religion, being human. He brought with him a boy, about a year old. Hidden in a pouch like batik cloth, tied to his chest. The boy has an identical twin. The wife and his older twin son couldn't get onto the vessel on time as cannons never stop pounding during the escape. At this point, Dhol seemed confused. He pursed his lips repetitively. He's not sure. To cry, to scream, to be angry. Dhol kept looking to the grave.   Is this for real?

Luqman continued, "We arrived in Hormuz about a month later. But he, having suffered chest infection, succumbed a few months on. I raised his son as mine, for I have none. I have lost a dear sifu, guru, ustaz, adviser, all in him. I wouldn't have become who I am today for not of his deeds." Dhol listened with even more questions lingering in his mind. What has all this got to do with me? Or is this Ayah's grave? Where is my twin? What happened to him? Are all these just coincidences that they fall in all the right places? And coming in sequences? Dhol can't speak out. Everything seemed swollen into his chest. His heartbeat, its pounding super hard feels like. He can hear eezzing sound in his ears. The world felt spinning. Dhol just collapsed flat on his face.

Chapter 26 - New Lifeline

The fall gave Dhol with a new shiny blue lump on his right forehead, also some scratches. It was almost dusk when Dhol came back to life, conscious from coma. Many hours since Luqman had Dhol on his lap throughout his passing out. Obviously, he couldn't carry Dhol of such weight, at his age of seventies. The turban was the only shade Luqman relied on to protect them both from direct heat. They were lucky to have a leather water pouch they brought along. That helped the least to quench their thirst, and certainly for survival.

Dhol cleared his throat, " So,….". Luqman interjected, " Yes, it's true. You have finally met your father. And that indeed was his grave. I am truly sorry that I have taken too long to find you, but glad to have this opportunity to relate them all."

"This tiny book that you have been carrying along, you must have search for it since at Adam's Peak. I read it all. And yes, Sam is your younger twin brother. He too sensed it. Karl found you. He told Sam of your lookalike from the very moment they found you by the beach. You never had the chance to know how he looks like. You both had the same birth marks on the right shoulder blade. Your dad told me. You will meet Sam again soon. Sam was the one who gave me this," while handing the book back to Dhol, who was still on his lap. Dhol woke up and sat up slowly, holding his forehead in pain, apart from all the confusion. He looked at the grave. Don't know how to react. Tears flow freely. He moved closer to the tombstone, held it for moments, and began to wail unconsolably. Luqman moved closer, rubbed Dhol's back hoping he could sooth him. Alas, let it go.

The sun set felt slower that day. The two men remained intact at the cemetery.

The sail across straits of Hormuz felt like a breeze. From a far east side of the vessel, Ayah's cemetery site remained in Dhol's sight. It's been several days now having spent time at Ayah's final resting place. He never had the opportunity to enjoy being in his dad's arms. He never knew how he looks like, other than the descriptions told by Umi. Dhol was glad at how events throughout the journey had turn out to be. He never would have expected it this way.

"Ayah and Umi, may your souls be placed among those closest to the righteous. Rest in Jannah, and in peace. Aamiin," Dhol held his hands both for a while longer in silence.

But Sam is a new chapter. There is a lifeline to look up to. Will Sam accept him?   Dhol recalled his many days and weeks and months of close encounters with Sam. Dhol truly felt strange every time they were within close range. The way Sam walks, talks, moves. Even his voice, height, features, and thoughts. They are similar to him. But little did it crossed his mind that Sam could be his long- lost twin brother. What actually happened to Sam? Why is he said to be from Nepal?

Chapter 27 - From Dol the Dhol to Abdullah

Dhol and Luqman secured their sea travel with breeze across the Hormuz Straits. The midsize boat of just Luqman and him, along with with the boat peddler was of least trouble. He felt the waves were very compromising for his trip, so smooth that continue northwest across the Jazirah in no time. They reached the port across the straits, and there, awaited their transport towards Mecca. As for the land journey across Arabian Peninsular, it was the weather, heat, wind and sandstorm were challenges of patience and perseverance.

"I have travelled on 4 occasions to Mecca for my pilgrimage and umrah. And throughout my journeys, it was this dromedary, also called the Arabian camel, that was humble enough to carry me. The dromedary is the tallest of the three species of camel, with large, even-toed ungulate with one hump on its back," explained Luqman, pointing to the camels they were on.

The men got down from their camels. They had earlier in their journey, stopped by at nearby village of Bir Ali to put on their white two pieces un-woven cloth, a change from their attire that they had been wearing throughout their travel. For the Muslims, to perform the rituals of Haj [pilgrimage] and Umrah [partial Haj], one of the conditions is to put the 2 pieces white clothes on at a location just prior to entering the city. A symbol that all men are equal, and that no one is of higher ranks than another.

As they approach the city, from the hilltop where the men stood, Mecca looked like a valley surrounded by hard rocks. In the middle, there stood a cube-shaped black structure. Entrance to the city was gained through four gaps in the surrounding mountains. Despite the distance, movements of human walking anticlockwise around the Kaabah is visible.

The heat of some 45 degrees celcius had the earth surface in a distance seen like mirage. No wind.

Dhol had mixed feelings. Too many fears, concerns, questions circling in his head. Biting his lips, Dhol in deep thoughts.

"My son, I can sense that you have a lot in mind right now. But first thing first. As you enter Mecca, priority must be to perform Umrah. It is appreciation ritual of thanks to Allah. A sign of respect. Inside that mosque of Masjidil Al Haram, lies the Kaaba, the centre of the earth. A central direction point for all Muslims when performing prayers."

The two men strolled down the higher grounds heading towards the city from south eastern side. Luqman continued, "But remember, it is not to that black stone that we are praying, seeking for forgiveness. The stone is just a stone. The stone was constructed by prophet Adam, reconstructed by prophet Abraham and his elder son, Ishmael, after the big flood had wipe-washed it during the great flood of prophet Noah's generation. The stone was no god. Unlike the pagans and others that worship their own creations. Praying towards the direction of the stone is a symbol of unity of all mankind from every angle of the earth. "

"Performing circumambulation around the Kaaba in anticlockwise direction has its scientific explanation as well," Luqman clarified further, gripping his right hand with the thumb pointing upwards. "Continuous rotating movements in anticlockwise direction will create positive currents. And as the current moves up, it sends positive vibes of do'a and prayers and hope and wishes to the above."

The men rode on their camels for another hour and reached their destination on time for the call of mid-day prayer, [the azan for zohor]. For generations, Meccan inhabitants had abided the respect of each prayers by stopping all activities and conduct prayers together. All worldly engagements can continue again right after. Hence, any visitors must adopt the rules and principles of the city too, just as its residences.

Dhol and Luqman were fortunate to have been at the right place, at the right time for the prayer. They hurried to get themselves through the crowds entering the mosque, reaching the front most row facing the huge black stone, and followed the Imam steps of prayers. AllahuAkbar.

As they completed their prayers, Dhol followed Luqman to make way for other worshippers to begin their circumambulation surrounding the Kaaba. The men moved some 20 feet away to make their do'a. Dhol, for now, had reached another of his life milestone achievements by saying his prayers right at the front of the holy place. He then was whisked by Luqman to perform the Tawaaf, the walk rotating around the Kaaba seven times, while saying prayers of thanks to Allah, seeking forgiveness, and reciting do'a for all his wishes to come to a reality. Seven as in seven hierarchies of heaven, seven as in seven layers of the earth, seven as in whatever that is between them, as ascribed in Al Quran Al Isra' 17:44:

تُسَبِّحُ لَهُ ٱلسَّمَٰوَٰتُ ٱلسَّبْعُ وَٱلْأَرْضُ وَمَن فِيهِنَّ ۚ وَإِن مِّن شَىْءٍ إِلَّا يُسَبِّحُ بِحَمْدِهِۦ وَلَٰكِن لَّا تَفْقَهُونَ تَسْبِيحَهُمْ ۗ إِنَّهُۥ كَانَ حَلِيمًا غَفُورًا ﴿٤٤﴾

"The seven heavens and the earth and whatever is in them exalt Him. And there is not a thing except that it exalts [Allah] by His praise, but you do not understand their [way of] exalting. Indeed, He is ever Forbearing and Forgiving."

They then moved on to the Safa hill, a location to the east of the Kaaba, to perform the next steps of Sai'e, a brisk walk or light run ritual between the hills of Safa and Marwa while reciting prayers and do'a. There, the ritual steps was adopted as a symbol of the struggles of Hajar, the mother of prophet Ishmael, in search of drinking water for the newly born son, Ishmael. It was during the plight of struggles of Hajar running between the two hills that she saw water began to flow from the grounds beneath where Ishmael was placed. She started digging deeper and water flowed out more from

the ground. They named it the ZamZam water.
They never got thirst again thereafter. It was
Allah's gift to mankind at a location where
water was so scarce. ZamZam well never dried
even until today, since some five thousand
years ago, the era of prophet Ishmael.

The hours of prayers felt short, while several
men had been observing Dhol and Luqman for
some time now. They had noticed Dhol and
Luqman completing their walks between Sai'e at
the Marwa hills when they approached Dhol.
"Assalamualaikum, ya Dhuyufurrahman [Guests
of the Merciful]," greeted the voice. Dhol was
speechless, but expected. He recognized the
voice. He has heard it before. He had always
wanted to hear that voice again. A
doppelganger stood among two others at the
corner of the Marwa hilltop, a few feet away
from Dhol and Luqman. The man went to
Luqman, bowed and kissed Luqman's hands and
hugged him. "Ayah," said the man. They held
there for a while, hugging each other tightly. No
words uttered momentarily. The rest of the
men stood still, observing from far. As they
began to loosen, Luqman turned to Dhol. "My

son, I bring you, your long-lost younger twin brother, Sam."

In Dhol's mind, flashbacks of moments are playing in his memory. The Pak Syeikh's green eyes that PakSu told him about. His lost and found note book being handed back by Luqman. A glimpse of Master Sam from the window in Danoshkodi Port.
 As Dhol and Sam held in each other arms, Dhol felt an indescribable deep feeling in gratitude of the whole episode in his life that he had to go through. From having lost a father whom he practically never met, never had a chance to enjoy his youth life with his twin, being raised in disguise as a commoner, witnessed the downfall of a civilization right in front of his very eyes, and to having lost his beloved mother, the love of his life. Yet, Allah has arranged for him a path that will lead him for a greater mission. And along with his long-lost twin brother, a newly adopted father, friends of brotherhood, and an opportunity to create and contribute for a better world. Aamiin

 Al Quran: Ad-Dhuha 93:7-8

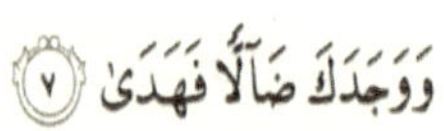

وَوَجَدَكَ ضَآلًّا فَهَدَىٰ ﴿٧﴾

"And He found you lost and guided [you],"

وَوَجَدَكَ عَآئِلًا فَأَغْنَىٰ ۝

"And He found you poor and made [you] self-sufficient."

Chapter 28 - A year on

A year later.....................

On the vessel Noah....... 7 men on a voyage around the world in their quest for greater good to mankind [Luqman 31:31]:.

أَلَمْ تَرَ أَنَّ ٱلْفُلْكَ تَجْرِى فِى ٱلْبَحْرِ بِنِعْمَتِ ٱللَّهِ لِيُرِيَكُم مِّنْ ءَايَٰتِهِۦٓ إِنَّ فِى ذَٰلِكَ لَءَايَٰتٍ لِّكُلِّ صَبَّارٍ شَكُورٍ ﴿٣١﴾

"Do you not see that ships sail through the sea by the favour of Allah that He may show you of His signs? Indeed, in that are signs for everyone patient and grateful."

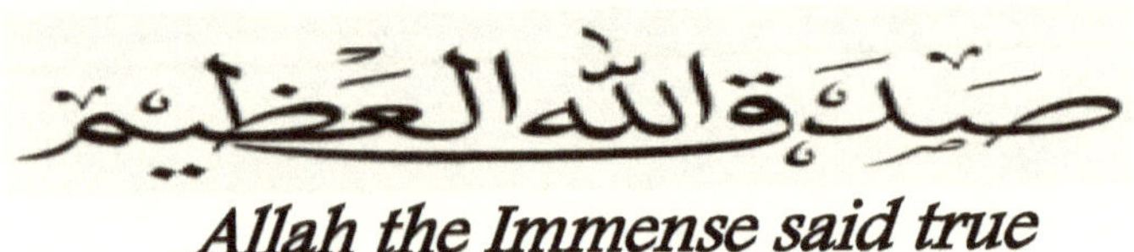

Allah the Immense said true

THE END

Glossary of Definitions

1. Assalamualaikum - Arabic language greeting meaning " Peace be upon you" that had been used for generations by both Muslims and non-Muslims in most Arabic speaking nations.
2. Hyper-startled - type of rare disorder response characterised by exaggerated startle
3. Serendip Island - Old name for Ceylon and later Sri Lanka
4. Ibu - Malay language term for "mother"
5. Syuruk - Period of the day after the end of morning / dawn prayer until the sun is about waist high
6. Lemang - Traditional Malay food made of glutinous rice cooked in a hallowed bamboo tube lined with banana leaves in order to prevent the rice from sticking to the bamboo. The rice grain is also mixed with coconut milk, salt and water. Lemang is usually only served on festivities due to its tedious preparation and it requires many hours of consistent heating to make it evenly cooked.

7. Rendang - Malay traditional spice meat dish cook with beef, coconut milk, spices, condiments

8. Ramadhan - 9th month of the Muslim calendar where all adult Muslims are to fast from dawn to dusk for the whole month.

9. Baju Melayu - Malay traditional costume for men

10. Chapal - Malay traditional leather skin slipper for men. It is usually worn by the upper class or warriors. Chapal is a slip in shoes with a hook in between the toes.

11. Baju Kurung - Traditional Malay dress for women

12. Pilgrimage - A series of ritual acts of worship. For the Muslims, pilgrimage to Mecca is the 5th pillars of Islamic faith. A duty for every adult Muslim to undertake, if they are able, and at least once in a life time.

13. Abang - Malay term for "elder brother"

14. Do'a - prayer, supplication, a request for help from Allah

15. Quill - a type of writing instrument like pens where it is a cut from the feather of a bird like a goose using a knife. The tip of the pen is dipped in ink. It works the same way as a modern fountain pen.

16. Subhan'Allah - Arabic meaning "God is Perfect" and free from any errors or defects

17. Tawaf - Arabic language meaning Circumambulation. Taken from 2 Latin words "circum" around and "ambulātus" to walk. It is the act of moving around a sacred black stone named Kaaba, which is located in the middle of the Grand Mosque in Mecca.

18. Subuh - Arabic and Malay languages meaning dawn

19. Syaitan - satan

20. Firaun - Pharoah

21. Tasbih - beads used for counting of recitations of prayers to god. It can be used by anybody but commonly used by Muslim religious men and women to count the number of recitations during rituals and after prayers.

22. Canai bread - Indian type bread made from flour and blended with ghee

23. Umat - Arabic language meaning community

24. Sahabat - "Close Friend" in Arabic and Malay languages

25. Sirah - derived from the Arabic in reference of the life and journey of Prophet Muhammad Rasullullah.

26. Sejadah - prayer mat.

References

1. The story of Prophet Daud https://wikisi.wordpress.com/2015/11/22/stories-of-the-prophets-davud-a-s/
2. HIdden Messages in Water by Masaru Emoto, David A. Thayne (Translator) <https://www.goodreads.com/book/show/33335.Hidden_Messages_in_Water
3. Anticlockwise https://lifeinsaudiarabia.net/blog/2018/03/15/why-the-tawaf-around-the-holy-kaaba-is-performed-anticlockwise-8-reasons/
4. Conversation between Roman's Heraclius and Abu Sufyan ibni Abbas http://www.sacred-texts.com/isl/bukhari/bh1/bh1_05.htm
5. Battle of the Trench *(The Life of Muhammad, Cairo, 1935)* <https://www.al-islam.org/restatement-history-islam-and-muslims-sayyid-ali-ashgar-razwy/battle-trench>
6. Extracted in full from the Byzantine Empire [610-641] http://saudigazette.com.sa/article/530524. Hadith narrated by Abdullah bin Abbas
7. All English translations of surahs quoted from Al Quran are using sahih international translation website at https://quran.com/78

Prologue

Dhol had just completed his Asar prayers.

Dhol folded his prayer mat and slide it under a bundle of sarong hanged at the cloth hanger next to his closet.

He turned to look at the parrot in its cage, located at his house balcony from his window.

The parrot seemed to be reciting the exact same words, verbatim from his prayers as if the parrot knows what the recitations meanings were.

Dhol shook his head. " True and brainy mankind should not be like you, parrot. Reciting words without a single clue what they meant." he uttered.

Some distance across the road, Dhol peeped deeply towards the building with a dome as its central structure, from his little hut, observing men walking out from the madrasah.

"If they too have not understood what they were reciting, then they are no different than you, our little friend here", he said to himself.

"I have and will continue to share what I have learned, only for the benefit of all."

Dhol flipped through a small book that he had been carrying with him wherever he goes for the past 15 years, ever since he started travelling half the globe.

Some scriptures in Malay, Sanscript, Arabic, Persian.

This is the gift I received. My gift to others too, regardless of who they are........while he walked towards the building across the road.

Sneek peek into the coming releases............

1. The Family Tree
2. Abraham – His Vison and Legacy
3. Yusuf & Musa – The Mapping

The Family Tree

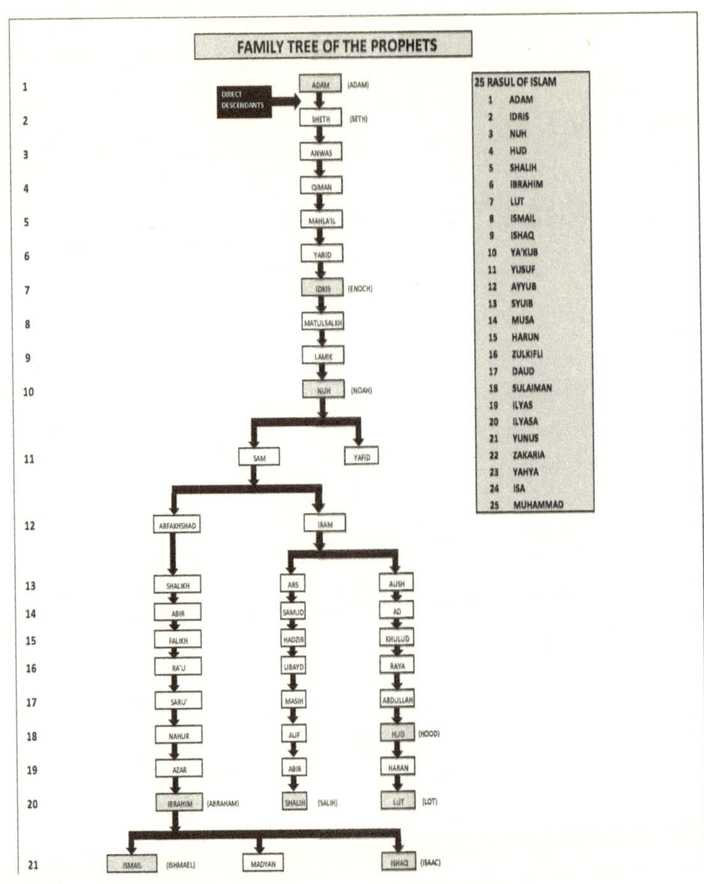

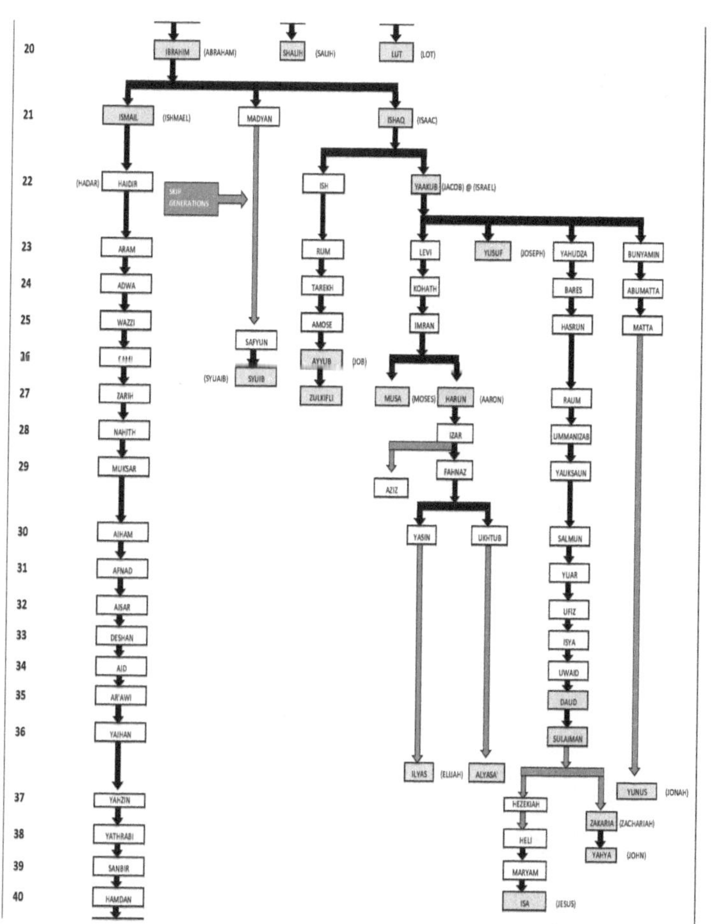

20
IBRAHIM (ABRAHAM)
SHALIH (SALIH)
LUT (LOT)
21
ISMAIL (ISHMAEL)
MADYAN
ISHAQ (ISAAC)
22
[HADAR] HAIDIR
SKIP GENERATIONS
ISH
YAAKUB (JACOB) @ (ISRAEL)
23
ARAM
RUM
LEVI
YUSUF (JOSEPH)
YAHUDZA
BUNYAMIN
24
ADWA
TAREKH
KOHATH
BARES
ABUMATTA
25
WAZZI
AMOSE
IMRAN
HASRUN
MATTA
26
ESHI
SAFYUN
AYYUB (JOB)
27
ZARIH
(SYUAIB) SYUIB
ZULKIFLI
MUSA (MOSES)
HARUN (AARON)
RAUM
28
NAHITH
IZAR
UMMANIZAB
29
MUKSAR
AZIZ
FAHNAZ
YAUKSAUN
30
AIHAM
YASIN
UKHTUB
SALMUN
31
AFNAD
YUAR
32
AJSAR
UFIZ
33
DESHAN
ISYA
34
AID
UWAID
35
AR'AWI
DAUD
36
YAIHAN
SULAIMAN
ILYAS (ELIJAH)
ALYASA'
YUNUS (JONAH)
37
YAHZIN
HEZEKIAH
ZAKARIA (ZACHARIAH)
38
YATHRABI
HELI
YAHYA (JOHN)
39
SANBIR
MARYAM
40
HAMDAN
ISA (JESUS)

40 HAMDAN
ISA (JESUS)
41 AD-DA'A
42 UBAID
43 ABQAR
44 AID
45 MAKHI
46 NAHISH
47 JAHIM
48 TABIKH
49 YADLAF
50 BILDAS
51 HAZA
52 NASHID
53 AWWAM
54 OBAI
55 QAMWAL
56 BUZ
57 AWS
58 SALAMAN
59 HUMAISI'
60 ADD
61 ADNAN
62 MA'AD
63 NIZAR
64 MUDAR
65 ELIAS
66 MUDRIKAH
67 KHUZAIMAN
68 KINANA
69 AN-NADR
70 MALIK
71 FAHR QURAISH
72 GHALIB
73 LO'I
74 KA'AB
75 MURRA
76 KILAB
77 QUSAI
78 ABDUL MANAF
79 HASHIM
80 ABDUL MUTALIB
81 ABDULLAH
82 MUHAMMAD (MOHAMMAD)

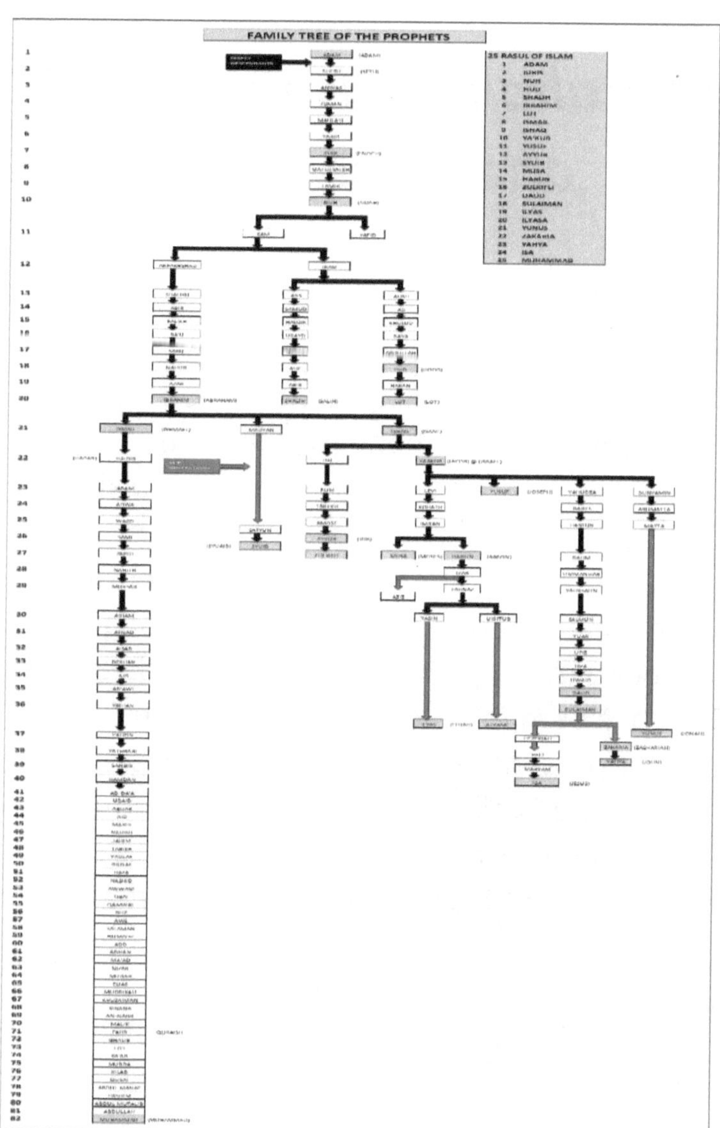

FAMILY TREE OF THE PROPHETS
25 RASUL OF ISLAM
1   ADAM
2   IDRIS
3   NUH
4   HUD
5   SHALIH
6   IBRAHIM
7   LUT
8   ISMAIL
9   ISHAQ
10 YA'KUB
11 YUSUF
12 AYYUB
13 SYUIB
14 MUSA
15 HARUN
16 ZULKIFLI
17 DAUD
18 SULAIMAN
19 ILYAS
20 ILYASA
21 YUNUS
22 ZAKARIA
23 YAHYA
24 ISA
25 MUHAMMAD

Abraham - His Vision and Legacy

Master Sam planned to fill the remaining days sharing with the small group of his portion of knowledge. He has many to pick from. Especially from his favourite Ustaz: Syeikh Nouman. In fact, he would narrate them verbatim, as in word by word. He remembered them well, as if fresh from his class though it had been many years ago. Once, he asked for Syeikh Nouman's blessing to adopt the Syeikh's style of presenting. Syeikh was a humble man. Though the Syeikh didn't reply to his request, Master Sam wishes and believes that his Syeikh would consent his scholar's wish to spread the words of Allah for the benefit of mankind.

Master Sam started with the father of all modern prophets.

That night came: and master Sam narrated.......

"Abraham has two children, Ishmael being the eldest, and Ishaq the younger.

We are going to first focus on Ishaq, who is also a prophet.

Ishaq has a son named Jacob, who is also a prophet. So practically, the descendants of Abraham via the Ishaq lineage has a continuous generation of prophets.

And Jacob has a nickname, Israel. Jacob has 12 children whom later on famously known as the twelve sons of Israel.

And each of the sons have big families, and each family eventually became prophets. They were later known as the twelve tribes of Israel.

Among the prominent prophets from the Israel lineage were Yusuf [Josef], Moses, Aaron, David, Solomon, and Jesus.

On the other hand, the elder son, Ishmael, who has a child, we don't know who, and grandchild, we don't know, and that continuous.

And lots of generations went by, without any prophets. Nothing is going-on on Ishmael's side

But a lot of going-on on Ishaq's side. The score is really on Ishaq's side. Zero on Ishmael later generations.

Every time a prophet dies on Ishaq's side, a new prophet was born and takes over.

Not a single generation in the entire history of the Israel where there were no prophets leading the civilization.

Now, because they got so many prophets on their side, and nothing from the Ishmael's, despite being their uncle, children of
Israel
they assume that every time a prophet is sent, it will come from Bani Israel.

It is only natural that when you get something a lot, you would stop appreciating it.

If you eat meat every day, then meat is no big deal.

If you eat meat only on your festive day in a year, that would truly means a lot and a big deal.

First thing happens when you get something too often, you don't take care of it.

The next thing happen is that you ignore them.

And things get really bad, sometimes they even kill the prophets.

Not only that, the children of Israel even made lies about prophets. They called Jesus's mother a whore.

And these were then re-written into their sacred book, according to their whims and fancies.

Bringing back the focus to the older son, Ismael is based in Mecca.

In the meantime, nothing is happening on Ishmael's side. They have been on vacation for a long time.

Abraham was responsible for putting this building together, pointing to the large black cube structure in front of them.

And this he did along with his older son, Ishmael

As they finished building, they both make a prayer to the AlMighty Creator, together. And that was told in the following verses.

AlQuran Al-Baqarah 2:127-129

وَإِذْ يَرْفَعُ إِبْرَٰهِۦمُ ٱلْقَوَاعِدَ مِنَ ٱلْبَيْتِ وَإِسْمَٰعِيلُ رَبَّنَا تَقَبَّلْ مِنَّآ إِنَّكَ أَنتَ ٱلسَّمِيعُ ٱلْعَلِيمُ ﴿١٢٧﴾

"And [mention] when Abraham was raising the foundations of the House and [with him] Ishmael, [saying], "Our Lord, accept [this] from us. Indeed You are the Hearing, the Knowing.""

رَبَّنَا وَٱجْعَلْنَا مُسْلِمَيْنِ لَكَ وَمِن ذُرِّيَّتِنَآ أُمَّةً مُّسْلِمَةً لَّكَ وَأَرِنَا مَنَاسِكَنَا وَتُبْ عَلَيْنَآ إِنَّكَ أَنتَ ٱلتَّوَّابُ ٱلرَّحِيمُ ﴿١٢٨﴾

"Our Lord, and make us Muslims [in submission] to You and from our descendants a Muslim nation [in submission] to You. And show us our rites and accept our repentance. Indeed, You are the Accepting of repentance, the Merciful."

رَبَّنَا وَٱبْعَثْ فِيهِمْ رَسُولًا مِّنْهُمْ يَتْلُوا۟ عَلَيْهِمْ ءَايَٰتِكَ وَيُعَلِّمُهُمُ ٱلْكِتَٰبَ وَٱلْحِكْمَةَ وَيُزَكِّيهِمْ ۚ إِنَّكَ أَنتَ ٱلْعَزِيزُ ٱلْحَكِيمُ ﴿١٢٩﴾

"Our Lord, and send among them a messenger from themselves who will recite to them Your verses and teach them the Book and wisdom and purify them. Indeed, You are the Exalted in Might, the Wise."

Their do'a specifically asked for:
One single messenger, one nation, one reference point, one constitution
How many messengers was sent on the other side [Ishaq]? Numerous, almost every generation.
How many messengers was sent to this side [Ishmael]? Only one, but the weight of this messenger is greater than all the messengers sent to the other side, as in all of them put together.
This messenger, Muhammad it was.
Back to the Kaaba, having no prophet for such extremely long time, the community began to worship idols despite Kaaba remained as a place for prayers.
It has been way too long that the true believers and its followers have died that none understands the teachings any clearer than just doing what their ancestors did.

But sadly, without any knowledge of the reasons behind such acts.

Back to the Ishaq family line, the last prophet sent was Isa [Jesus].
Israelites were bad to most prophets. Yet they were worst to Isa. Right from when he was a baby that they insulted him and his mom.
A matter of fact, they even tried to kill Isa.
Now that after more than 600 years, not a single messenger arrived to continue the legacy.
As the final messenger was sent down, he was among the Arabs, not the Jewish Israelites community.
Bani Israel referred to their scriptures, and to their astonishment, it was true that Muhammad was clearly mentioned in both Torah and Injil.
This is not acceptable to Bani Israel. To them, all prophets should come from the Ishaq lineage.
As far as they are concerned, Ishmael was born by Siti Hajar, an Egyptian maid of Abraham.

Ishmael was regard as an illegitimate child. So, his descendants were considered haram.

Ishaq is the chosen child. Bani Israel is the chosen race and that prophets should only come from the same lineage.

And for a lot of centuries, there was no prophets sent to the other side. Hence no problem.

For generations, Bani Israel was given so much privileges and benefits. They screw things up. They disrespect they're own prophets.

The children of Israel even changed the contents of Torah and Bible. Words of Al Mighty was re-written.

Changes made to their likings, selecting only those they like and deleting the remaining.

All of a sudden, Muhammad arise to Ishmael's lineage as the final Messenger.

Sent to a location [Mecca] that no civilizations thought would be to interest of the great powers.

Romans were not interested, Persian didn't even wink at the Arabs.

Water is limited, trees very scarce, temperature of desert most of the year.

The only thing advance was the literature, Arabic literature, well known to the rest of the world.

Yusuf & Musa - The Mapping

When the group assembled after the night prayer, master Sam went straight to the point:

"In suratul Qasaas, Musa faces Firaun. In this surah, Firaun said to Musa," What you are telling us is nothing that we have ever heard before, and a made-up magic." Firaun was referring to the staff that turned into a snake and back, and was used to produce water. Firaun further said," we have never heard of this, we have never come across this from any of our ancestors during earliest of time". These words were uttered by Firaun in his parliament, in front of all his ministers, dignitaries and mighty armies' presence."

"Little did Firaun realized that his police chief was already a believer of Musa. The general stood up and said in response to Firaun," No doubt about it that Yusuf had come to the Egyptians before you. Remember that he came to you with clear proves too. And here we are rejecting Musa, but doesn't Musa reminded us of Yusuf?". He continued," And when he died, remember that you guys said that there is never going to be another messenger after him."

"I was searching for connections between surah Yusuf [12] and surah Al Qasaas [28]. But now I found that in surah Al Mukminun [40], the Egyptians themselves was telling us a clear connection between Musa and Yusuf. Look at how beautiful the arrangements in Al Quran that even the numberings are neatly placed to show relationship of each topics.

Let's explore further. "

"Surah Yusuf [12] covers largely about Yusuf. Surah Al Qasaas [28] talks greatly on Musa. Surah Yusuf begins with a father showing love to his son. Surah Al Qasaas begins with a mother showing love to his newly born son. When we read surah Yusuf, how come it did not mention about the mom. When we read surah Al Qasaas, it only talks about the dad. Looks like there is a dad story and a mom story. "

"Surah Yusuf portrays the dad spending time to listen to Yusuf, a show of love by paying attention by listening to someone. In this case, the son. On the other side, Al Qasaas describes physical love of a mom feeding the son and caressing him in her arms. "

"The story further relate that father tries to protect his son by warning him of not telling his dreams to others, not even his brothers. In surah Al Qasaas, the mom tries to protect her son by flowing him in a basket like container passing through the Nile river. In surah Yusuf, the dad protective measure is logical, but failed."

"The mom on the other hand, adopted the instructed illogical protective measure, but worked. We can learn from these events that human plans, and Allah has plan too. Our plan may be entirely logical, but fail. The illogical step that Allah instructed us to do, succeeded. But Allah has His way of fixing up plans, way beyond man's ability to foresee."

"The dad constantly advice his son Yusuf with advice and compliments. The mom constantly feed her new born Musa with milk. Both nourishments, knowledge and food, complete the picture."

"The dad loses his son, the mom loses her child too. The dad loses his son without his will. The mom loses his child willingly by putting him in a basket and flow it through the river."

"Yusuf was in danger as he might get drown in the well. Musa was in danger as he might get drown in the river. Yusuf's brothers asked the dad if they can take him along for a trip. On the other hand, the mom asked Musa's sister to go after him along the riverside. The brothers went out with evil intend. The sister, in accordance to her mother's instruction to protect in good intention. "

"The brothers came back to inform the dad, Yacob with a made-up story of Yusuf's tragic death, eaten by wild animal. On the contrary, the sister came back with a made-up story telling Firaun's wife that she knew of a family that could feed breast milk to Musa's liking. One story was made up to ensure the separation while the other causes the reunion in the family."

"Yusuf's dad was sad that the brothers wanted to take him along, and feared something bad may happen. In the case of Musa, Allah sends revelation to his mom to not be afraid and sad. "

"The family of Yusuf was reunited years later after going through hardship. The Musa family was reunited on the very same day. Yusuf's family was reunited by the government order much later upon Yusuf being appointed as the Treasury Minister of Egypt. Musa's family was reunited also by government's order from the Queen of Egypt."

"Let's compare their childhood. Yusuf was saved from a well and became a high ranked government official years later. Musa was saved from a river and became an adopted son of the King."

"When they both became teenagers, they were given specialties and wisdom. Yusuf was capable to interpret different kinds of dreams and speeches. Musa is smart and strong physically."

"They both ended up in the Egyptian palace. Yusuf as a servant and Musa as an adopted son."

"Yusuf is put to a test, an indoor test on lust and women. Musa is put to a test too, an outdoor fight involving strength. The tests are adultery for Yusuf and murder for Musa. Both are major crimes. And these are crimes that had always been the reasons to the fall of any civilizations. These examples are clearly written in the respective surah [12 & 28] and subsequently strengthen in Surah Al-

Mukmin[40]. It is so beautifully arranged that only those who observe will notice and acknowledge the greatness of how each verses and chapters in Quran is established."

"Now back to the story of Yusuf and Musa. "

"Yusuf did not commit the crime but was jailed, Musa committed a crime but he escaped. Yusuf's request was to prove his innocence, Musa came back and wanted to confess his guilt on his crime. Yusuf's words were taken seriously by the king. Musa was belittled and dismissed in every word he uttered."

"Yusuf was released by the king, wanted Yusuf to be his personal aide, exclusively for the king, as the king is fascinated by Yusuf's intelligence. On the contrary, the king [Firaun] wanted to personally kill Musa as he felt it was a mistake that he raised Musa who eventually revolt against him."

"Yusuf's helper is his brother, Benjamin. Likewise, Musa's helper is his brother, Aaron. Yusuf's brother is helpful by working but staying silent. Musa's brother speaks more and eloquently as compared to him. "

Disclaimer

While the storyline is a work of fiction, all the verses from Al Quran remain intact and accurate. The Sirah, as in historical journey of Prophet Muhammad and his companions, as well as narrations of all prophets are transcribed in accordance to records stated in either Al Quran or collections from quoted sources.

That being mentioned, all characters appearing in this work having any resemblance names, characters, places, incidents, living or dead are entirely coincidental.

DHOL

ISBN: 978-967-17640-0-8

Copyright © 2019 Solihin Yusoff

All rights reserved. No part of this publication may be reproduced, distributed, or transmitted in any form or by any means, including photocopying, recording, or other electronic or mechanical methods, without the prior written permission of the publisher, except in the case of brief quotations embodied in critical reviews and certain other non-commercial uses permitted by copyright law. For permission requests, write to the publisher, addressed "Attention: Permissions Coordinator," at the address below.

Solihin Yusoff Shah Alam 40100 Selangor
Malaysia

Copyright © 2019 Solihin Yusoff
All rights reserved

About the author

SOLIHIN YUSOFF

Born in Batu Gajah, Malaysia. Raised in Ipoh, his dad was an internal auditor and his mom, a school teacher, Solihin attended his lower primary education at St. Michael's Institution, Perak. Upon completing Malaysian Certificate of Education from MRSM Kulim, Solihin continued his higher education in Finance and Economics at Southern Illinois University, USA. He later completed his Masters of Science in Financial Economics.

Solihin never really took writing seriously until he left his corporate life. He spent almost half of his working life abroad as an expat for a leading multi-national corporation. Along with his wife, Ana, they raised their 5 children while being posted in several countries assigned. The children benefited a wide view of the world perspective by further advancing their education in different parts of the world.

Solihin was always as inquisitive and seeker in understanding the secrets of the Holy Script, The Quran. He spent full year in preparing for his pilgrimage while at the same time deepens his knowledge on the whats and whys in each steps of the rituals. It was during his visits to Mecca and Medina that he began collecting notes, books and details on historical importance.

Solihin was inspired with the likes of famous scholars such as Ustaz Nouman Ali Khan, Prof Dato MAZA of Perlis, prominent Ustaz Wan Hizam, and several local clerks as references for clarification, guidance, references, studies, and spiritual experiences.

Solihin travels the world in search of footsteps of Islam. He feels that it is one's obligation to share and spread the words of wisdom for the betterment of mankind.

Copyright © 2019 Solihin Yusoff
All rights reserved

DHOL
In a state of Confusion
SOLIHIN YUSOFF

www.ingramcontent.com/pod-product-compliance
Lightning Source LLC
Chambersburg PA
CBHW030307160726
47992CB00005B/1920